JOURNEY
OF HONOR
A LOVE STORY

Journey of Honor, A Love Story By Jaclyn M. Hawkes
Copyright © August 2010 All Rights Reserved

Published & Distributed by:

Granite Publishing & Distribution, LLC
868 North 1430 West
Orem, UT 84057
801-229-9023   Toll Free 1-800-574-5779
Fax 801-229-1924
www.granitebooks.com

Cover Design By: Steve Gray
Page Layout and Design By: Michelle L. Elias

ISBN: 987-1-59936-059-1
Library of Congress Control Number: 2010931135
First Printing August 2010
10 9 8 7 6 5 4 3 2 1

Printed in the United States of America

DEDICATION

This book is dedicated to courageous pioneers everywhere, both past and present, who quietly do whatever it takes. It's also dedicated to my sweet, hard working sister-in-law from Holland. She's the best thing that ever happened to my dorky brother and keeps him guessing with her linguistic twists. And, of course, this book is dedicated to my good husband. He makes me laugh, hugs me when I cry, and is the love of my life.

JOURNEY
OF HONOR
A LOVE STORY

JACLYN M. HAWKES

CHAPTER 1

WAYCROSS, GEORGIA 1844

Trace was still up and sitting in front of the fire thinking when his father, William, known locally as Doc Grayson, came back after spending the evening delivering a baby. He stowed his medical bag and joined Trace before the fire with a long sigh of contentment. "Perfect way to end a day. Meeting a brand new little spirit straight from heaven." His deep southern drawl fit his quiet, steady demeanor like a glove.

Trace looked up at him, but said nothing, still lost in his own thoughts. He loved his father dearly, but tonight there was restlessness upon him. Even hearing about the successful delivery couldn't shake it, in spite of the fact that he had spent years working to become a doctor himself. This day had been coming for a while now. He had known that eventually he would leave to make his own way in the world, but he didn't necessarily want it to be to avoid a girl. He had only been home from school in Pennsylvania for two days, but already he was fed up with the spoiled and obnoxious young daughter of their well-to-do plantation owner neighbor.

After several minutes of silence, Trace began. "Lucretia Tapp was here again today."

William nodded, "Was she rude to Mose again?"

Trace gave a snort of disgust. "When has she ever *not* been rude to Mose? She's treated him badly from the day you adopted him when we were seven. It was her own father that had beaten him unconscious, remember? He passed on his bigotry perfectly. She hates all Blacks on sight." He paused and added bitterly. "She hates them, but she could never have the life she has without their labor."

His father shook his head sadly. "This whole slavery issue will end someday. In the not too distant future I hope. In the mean time, I believe that it will be worse than ever. We southerners are a hard headed lot. I'm afraid you're not going to change her or her father's way of thinking."

Trace turned to him. "I don't want to change her. I just don't want anything to do with her at all. With either of them. What does she want with me anyway? She knows how I feel about slavery. We're absolute opposites. And she's sixteen. Why doesn't she set her heart on one of the men around here that would cow to her father and be willing to take over the plantation someday? There are certainly enough that would be willing to put up with her to have Papa's money waiting in the wings."

After considering this for a moment or two, William said, "You've hit it head on, Trace. You're the only one that is stronger than her father. That's why she admires you. Even though she's..." He hesitated. "Even though she doesn't seem to have much character, she respects yours."

Almost bitterly, Trace went on. "She didn't act like she respected me much today. She was all but throwing herself at me, and when I wasn't having any of it, she threatened to tell her father that I had behaved inappropriately so that he would insist that I make an honest woman of her." He shuddered. "Can you imagine waking up beside her for the rest of my life?" He finally grinned across at his father. "I'd have to resort to drinking if I were stuck like that."

William chuckled. "You would never resort to drinking, so you'd best not marry her." After another pause, he went on. "That being said, I'd hate for you to have to face Henry Tapp's shotgun because of Lucretia's lies. Being reasonable isn't one of his strong points."

"No, it isn't." Trace looked into the flames for a time. Finally, he said, "Mose is miserable here now. Losing Callie has

2

hit him hard. He hasn't smiled once since I've been back from school."

William rubbed his temple. "It truly was a horrible time. She was in labor for more than two days. I've never wished for greater medical knowledge in my life."

Quietly Trace replied, "The fact that it was her master's child that she died trying to deliver made it worse than ever. Mose is a wonderful, Christian man, but I think that he honestly struggles not to hate Tapp for that. I can hardly blame him. In his shoes, I'd feel the same way."

William didn't answer, but the sad look that he gave Trace made him think that his father knew where he was going with all this. Finally, Trace asked, "How have you done it all these years, Pa? How do you patiently keep patching up humans that another human being has beaten or starved or abused without becoming hopelessly bitter?"

His father looked over at him with the understanding of years in his eyes. "It's what I do, Trace. I am a healer. I could no more not take care of people that need help than fly. What's more, it's what you do as well. You are a physician to your soul. You just have enough of your mother's fire to want to fight back more than I ever did. And maybe that's a good thing.

"In fact I'm sure it is. This world needs good men that are willing to take a stand for what's right. It will be men like you that finally bring about the changes that are necessary to make the world a safer and happier place for those less fortunate. In a way, I envy your passion. All these years I have been content to be the best doctor that I could and leave the causes to others. I probably should have done more standing up for what is right in my lifetime."

Trace shook his head. "You have always worked to help people, Pa. You need have no regrets. But I'm afraid I'm not like you. I can't stand by and watch anymore. I want to go far enough away from all of this that I never hear the word slavery again in my life."

Meeting his son's eyes, William said, "Do what you have to do, Trace, but don't be fooled into believing that there isn't cruelty and bigotry anywhere that you might go. If it isn't slavery, it may be something else just as bad. I'm afraid that the devil controls the hearts of some men, no matter where they live or what color they are."

"I'm sure you're right, but right here and now I feel like I should go. Maybe someday I'll come back, but you're good for another thirty years here, and this community doesn't need more than one doctor. In the meantime, I need to go earn the money to finish the last year of school. I'm sure Mose wants to go away as well. Avoiding Lucretia is just a good excuse I suppose."

William stared into the flames of the fire until he finally said, "I'll miss you, Trace. Even though you're only twenty years old, you're already more educated and experienced than most of the doctors in this country. You've been the best son and medical apprentice that I could have ever asked for, and I've always been proud of you. I'm sure that I always will be.

"Your mother will be sad as well. We'll miss both of you this time if Mose goes with you, but you know what you need to do, and I wouldn't want to stop you. You have your whole life ahead of you, and much that needs to be experienced. Go if you must, but always remember that you have great potential. I know that you will always be honorable and good. Just don't let life's ups and downs make you forget that you are also great. Great men are hard to come by."

St. Joseph, Missouri July 10, 1848

Trace Grayson stepped out of the Robidoux Hotel, where he'd met with his friend and now wagon master John Sykes and looked around for Mose. He was supposed to be here somewhere, but so far... Trace's train of thought was interrupted by the appearance of the most striking young woman that he had ever seen. It wasn't just that she was beautiful, graceful, and well dressed. There was something in her bearing that, combined with the rest made her step onto the wooden boardwalk like she was the queen of all America.

She wasn't that tall, but seemed to be because of her almost regal bearing. Her blonde hair was done up somehow, and only cascades of curls could be seen under the hat that matched her tan traveling suit. Even in just drab tan, she couldn't help but appear colorful and vibrant. Trace watched her walk toward him down the boardwalk, he and all the rest of the people within sight of her. He almost shook himself to focus on what he was supposed to be doing. For just a moment he couldn't remember what that was exactly.

Mose. He was looking for Mose. They'd been waiting for several precious days to scrape up enough wagons to begin heading west on the trail to California, and John had just barely told him that he believed he had finally gotten the twenty wagon minimum that he'd been seeking to mollify the army. Trace and Mose had already been to California and back once this year and were now waiting to leave again with six more wagons of goods of their own to be taken and sold in the territories far to the west to be sold.

They'd made better money with every trip they'd taken across the trail in the last three years, and Trace had somewhat set his medical goals aside to enjoy being in business for himself. Being his own boss had done something for him. He was more confident now than he'd ever been after knowing that he could be successful in whatever he faced from coast to coast. This was the first time they'd tried two trips in one year, but they thought it was realistically possible if they could just get on the trail. Supposedly, whoever John had found was in the same hurry to leave and could be ready first thing in the morning; which was vital if they were to make it safely through the mountains in the west before the winter snows.

Thinking back on the beautiful girl that he'd just seen, he almost wished that they were still waiting. He'd never had a girl affect him like that. He'd almost wanted to walk right up to her and introduce himself and ask her to come west with them on the spot. He smiled at himself, a little embarrassed at the whole idea. He was still smiling when Mose rounded the corner from the blacksmith shop in front of him.

Mose looked at his expression and asked, "What are you so all fired happy about?"

Trace shook his head and grinned at him. "I saw a girl." He chuckled and admitted to his friend, "I almost asked her to marry me right there on the boardwalk. The only thing that stopped me was knowing that you needed me to make it across all those miles of trail. Am I loyal or what?"

Mose laughed. "Must have been some girl. To test your loyalty and all."

Still feeling a little silly because the smile was stuck on his face, Trace said, "She was. Blonde, slim and graceful. With these eyes! Blue so bright that I could see them clear down the boardwalk. And walks like royalty."

Glancing sideways at him, Mose laughed again. "Tarnation, Trace. This *really* must be some girl. I can't wait to see the female that has this kind of effect on an old lone wolf like you."

"I'm not a lone wolf. I've just never found the right one." He laughed at himself and brushed the whole situation off. "I'll probably never see her again. We'll be long gone in the morning. But, much as we've wanted to leave, I almost wish we were still delayed."

Sobering, Mose replied, "If this is really a big thing, other drivers can be found, man. You can stay here and we'll take the wagons across without you."

"What, and miss all the fun? Not a chance! I wouldn't miss all the dust and mud and lightning and flood swollen rivers and..."

"All right, all right. I get the idea. Enough of the palaver. You're going to make *me* decide not to go. Did Sykes have any news?"

Trace slapped his forehead. "I completely forgot to tell you. He got the last wagon. Some Dutch people. An older couple and their granddaughter in fact. He said they were Mormons. We're leaving at first light tomorrow. I'm surprised that John was willing to take a woman and child along, but he said that they wanted to go this year enough to pay him to let them come along. There are no other trains going this late, so they were as desperate as we are.

"John said that they seemed to be steady and dependable. The Mormons are supposedly a little weird, but I hear they're pretty quiet-living. At least we won't have to deal with any more rannies like the other teamsters that came on day before yesterday. Those boys are trouble."

Shaking his head again, Mose gave him a hard time. "You've clean lost your mind, boy. The news we've been waiting for and you almost forget to mention it. I wish I could have seen this girl. She must have had some amazing love potion or something."

Trace waved a gloved hand. "Naw. Give me a long stretch of nothing but dust and heat and my mind will come right back. I'll be fine."

They finished their last minute errands, and picked up the mule team that Mose had left at the blacksmith's to be shoed, and headed back to the rendezvous spot on the riverbank near the ferry. After rounding up their other five drivers, they cautioned them to be ready to roll at dawn. Then the two of them settled in to make dinner and get bedded down early. Tomorrow would be a big day.

Just before dark, another big Conestoga wagon rolled up and Trace and Mose watched the husband begin to unhitch. They went over to the wagon to say hello and lend a hand. Trace was just unbuckling the harness on the far mule when he heard the sound of women's voices. Turning, he looked toward the back of the wagon where there were two women walking toward him.

It was her. It took him a minute or two to get his mind to understand that the girl he'd seen was the granddaughter of the Dutch couple that would be traveling with them. He looked up and caught Mose's eye and nodded at the girl, and then almost laughed out loud when Mose made a perfect O with his lips. Their own personal brand of communication without speaking was interrupted by the wagon master approaching.

He pulled Trace and Mose along to the couple and the girl. "Oh, good. I see that you've already met." He turned to the Dutch man. "Josiah, these are the two young men that I was telling you about. Trace Grayson and Mose Brown. They and their men are the ones that you're going to want to travel near. Or my own drivers. They're much more respectable types than the other teamsters. The other ones aren't going to be all that pleasant for your women folk I'm afraid. Stick near these two and you'll be fine." Turning back towards Trace and Mose he said, "You two keep an eye out for them, will you?"

Grinning, Mose said, "Shore, we'll keep an eye out for them Sykes, but we've only met Josiah here. We haven't had the pleasure of meeting the women."

Trace was still a little thunderstruck about traveling with the girl, but he stepped forward and took the women's hands smoothly as Josiah introduced them with a thick Dutch accent. "This is my wife Petja VanKomen and my granddaughter Giselle VanKomen. They are goot women and we are grateful to have some respectable men to travel with. *Bedankt*. Thank you."

"It will be our pleasure I'm sure, sir." Trace met Giselle's eyes. "We've never had the good fortune of traveling with such lovely ladies." He could almost swear that she wanted to roll her eyes when he said it and he grinned at her. "Welcome aboard."

"Thank you." Her accent was milder than her grandfather's and her hand shook his honestly without any of the flirtatiousness that women often used to greet him with. "Tell me, are you Mr. Grayson or Mr. Brown?"

"Grayson. Please, call me Trace. There is certainly no need to stand on ceremony in a wagon train. And this is my brother, Mose Brown." She raised her eyebrows as she tipped her head to take in Mose standing beside him, black and three inches over Trace's six foot one. Trace grinned again and said, "He's adopted."

She laughed a pretty laugh, filled with sincere humor, as she moved to take Mose's hand. "So I see. It's nice to meet you, Mr. Brown."

He cleared his throat. "You'd best call me Mose, ma'am. Trace is right, and if you call me Mr. Brown I won't have any idea who you're talking to." He flashed her a wide smile that gleamed white against his dark chocolate skin. "You need anything, you just holler. We'll hep you right out."

"Thank you. I may do just that. I'm afraid I'm new to this wagon train travel. I have a great deal to learn."

Josiah put his arm around her. "You'll do just fine, Elle. You always do. I'm sure you'll learn fast."

After the brief introduction, Trace, Mose and John went back to their own respective camps. Once out of hearing of their Dutch neighbors, Mose turned to look at Trace with a grin. "You had enough of your mind to remember your name back there. I'm right proud of you, Trace. Now if you can just remember how to harness and drive a team, we may be okay this trip."

"She's even prettier close up than I thought. We may honestly be in trouble here, Mose. I'll probably forget which end the harness goes on." He went back to cooking with a sigh. "How are we ever gonna keep our teamsters focused on traveling?"

An hour later, as they were cleaning up and rolling out their beds, there came a small cavalcade of horsemen to their camps. Looking up, Trace caught the eye of the Sheriff in the lead. He and Trace and Mose had known each other for three years, having met on their first trip through St. Joe. Trace had actually helped put the Sheriff back together after being shot when the regular doctor had been out of town. Apparently, Trace had done a far better job than the regular doctor and the Sheriff had tried to talk them into staying in town permanently.

On seeing him, the Sheriff came right over and gripped his hand. "Trace, didn't know you were part of this train. It's good to see you again. You can't be talked into staying here yet, can you? We'd still love to have you."

Trace smiled at him, but the smile died right out when he saw who the Sheriff's companion was. Trace addressed him without extending his hand, which the Sheriff picked right up on. "Filson. What brings you to St. Joe? I thought St. Louis was your town. You coming to swindle the people here now? What, did they catch on to you in St. Louis?"

There was no welcome in his voice whatsoever. He turned to the Sheriff. "Jim, you're in poor company here. What's a good man like you doing with a crook like this?" There was disgust in his eyes that Filson glared at, but didn't challenge.

Filson turned to the Sheriff. "Ignore this man, Sher'f. He's just sore because he came out the loser in a business deal once."

"An underhanded, crooked business deal that you cooked up, Filson. If I'd known then what I know now, I wouldn't have touched a deal with you with a hundred-foot pole. At least I can say that I was honest with those people and made it right. That's a whale of a lot more than you can say." While they talked, Mose and four of their other men came up to Trace's side.

Obviously uncomfortable with this talk, the Sheriff tried to change the subject. "Have you got a young, Dutch girl traveling with you? Filson here says that she stole something from him. I'm here to arrest her."

Trace looked coolly at Filson. "Yes, she's here, but once you meet her, you'll never believe Filson's word over hers. She's as obviously honest as he is sneaky. Her wagon is right over here."

As a group, they headed to the VanKomen wagon where Trace spoke quietly to Josiah, asking that he get Giselle to come out. Josiah's glance hardened when he saw Filson. Apparently he was familiar with Filson's character as well. He called her out and Trace was surprised to see this proud and confident young

10

woman pale visibly when she saw Filson. Trace gave her a hand to climb down from the wagon and she immediately moved to stand behind his shoulder away from Filson.

Filson's gaze was sickening as he looked Giselle over, and Mose moved closer to Trace in front of her while their men fanned out on both sides of them. Filson immediately turned to the Sheriff. "That's her Sher'f. She's the one that done took my money. Come right into my hotel room. I saw her leaving as I came up the hall, but I couldn't catch her. She went down the back stairs." Filson gave Giselle a disgusting grin and she raised her head almost proudly to address the Sheriff.

"That is a lie! I have never taken anything from this man and I would not want to! I haven't even been in a hotel here in this town. We've been here only yesterday and today and I have only been in the general store and the Chinaman's cafe. My grandparents can assure you that I tell the truth."

Filson sneered, "She's lying. She took it. I saw her. Take her in, Sher'f."

The Sheriff turned to Filson and said brusquely, "I'll thank you to let me handle my job, Filson." Turning to Giselle, he gently said, "I'm sorry, miss. I'm afraid that I'll have to take you in until I get to the bottom of this."

At this point John Sykes walked up and Trace asked, "How long will that take, Jim? We were heading out at dawn trying to make it to California before it snows."

Filson smiled wickedly. "Too bad, Grayson! You'll be leaving without one little, Dutch thief. She stays here to serve her time and return my money!"

The Sheriff turned on Filson. "That's enough! You aren't making any decisions here. Let me do my job. In fact," he turned to his deputy, "Walt, take him back into town with you while I finish up here."

Filson started to protest, but the Sheriff raised a hand to stop him, and then turned his back to him to address Trace. He glanced back at Filson who had yet to leave, and at the Sheriff's pointed look, Filson finally turned and followed the deputy.

When he was well away, the Sheriff turned to Trace. "On second thought, Grayson. I don't want to haul this girl in on that snake's word. Would you be willing to be responsible for her until the morning when I can get to the bottom of this?"

Trace glanced back at Giselle. "Is that okay with you, Miss VanKomen?"

She nodded. "Yes. Certainly." She turned to the Sheriff. "How much money does he say I have stolen?"

"Two hundred dollars."

Giselle looked horrified. "That's a lot of money! What do we have to do in the morning before I can go?"

Scratching his head, the Sheriff looked uncomfortable. "I'm not sure exactly. Filson is really kicking up a fuss. He's insisting that I not let you leave until I have a trial, but so far I have no evidence except his word. I'll know better in the morning after I can question some people. I'll let you know as soon as I can. In the meantime, stay where Trace can keep an eye on you." With that he turned to go.

There was silence for a few moments after he left and then Giselle looked up at Trace. "I have stolen nothing. I give you my promise. I will be in my grandfather's wagon." She turned and went back to the rear of the wagon again and he heard her long sigh as she went.

Josiah turned to John Sykes and said, "My granddaughter is honest and she has been with my wife and me every moment, but I'm afraid if they insist that she stay that we must too. I'm sorry to disappoint you, but we must stay with her. Henry Filson is a horrible man and he can't be allowed to get near her. If she can't go in the morning, then neither can we. Please forgive us." He turned on his heel and walked away, leaving John and Trace and Mose staring at each other in disappointed disgust. The other men headed back to their bedrolls while the three of them tried to think of a solution to the mess that might cost them their whole trip.

Finally, Trace said, "I'm going into town to talk to Jim and find out what our options are." He turned to go get his horse where it was picketed. When he returned to the fire, both Mose and John had their horses as well and the three of them swung into their saddles and headed out at a trot. At the Sheriff's office, they found Filson, still storming around, mad that they hadn't dragged Giselle in and locked her up as he had demanded.

"You're going to let her get off without even checking into this, aren't you? I'm going to go over your head! I'll go to the governor if I have to! You're not going to get away with this just because she blinks those eyes and sways her hips a little. I demand that you treat her just like any other thief caught in the act!"

The Sheriff turned to the deputy again. "Walt, take his statement and find out if there is any other evidence, or witnesses. See if anyone else can remember seeing her in the hotel. Then get him outta here." He turned to the others. "Come into my office a minute would you?"

Once inside with the door shut, he looked at the three of them and shrugged his shoulders. "I'm not sure what this guy wants, but I think it has something to do with keeping her from going west. Hopefully, we'll have something more by morning."

Trace asked him right out. "What are our options, Jim? If she doesn't go, her grandparents won't either and they're a large part of our train. The army isn't going to let us leave without at least twenty wagons, and her grandfather is paying us to help them. Without them, we're stuck while our chance to make it past the mountains before the snow dwindles. What can we do to be able to take her? If we offer to put up a two hundred dollar bond that he can keep if you prove it was her, would that work?"

Sadly, Jim shook his head. "I doubt it. He wants her, not his money. I have to at least make a show of following the law."

"What if we left with provisions to bring her back if she's proven guilty and you send a rider for her?"

The Sheriff thought about that for a minute. "No... I'd have to have a more concrete guarantee that I could show him to keep him from raising a ruckus clear to the state capital. She

13

either has to stay until this is settled or you have to get Filson to give up trying to keep her here."

Mose was thoughtful. "What does he want her for? What's the reason that he doesn't want her to go west?"

Trace gave a disgusted sound. "You and I both know what he wants from her, Mose. You could see it in his face. You could see it in her face. She's apparently had dealings with him before. She was terrified of him."

The Sheriff looked at Trace. "You really believe that he thinks, if she doesn't leave, she'll agree to be with him?"

Trace shook his head. "Of course not. I don't think he cares if she agrees or not. I think he thinks that he can do as he pleases. We knew him in St. Louis, and he thought he was untouchable. He's got someone there with the law that lets him get away with running amok. And they're Mormons. Remember? You can do anything to a Mormon in this state and get away with it. The Governor himself signed an order that they should all be killed."

The Sheriff was appalled. "That's disgusting!"

Trace shrugged. "You saw him. He's disgusting. So what can we do to be able to take her?"

John joined in for the first time. "It sounds to me like what we need to do is to make her seem unattainable enough that Filson will let her go without a fuss."

All three of them turned towards him and the Sheriff asked, "What have you got in mind, John? I'd have to guard her night and day to keep her safe if what you think is true, and I haven't got that kind of man power. And the soonest we could hold a trial would be a few days at the least."

They were all silent for a time and then Mose said, "What if she was married? Could you let her go if we personally guaranteed that we'd bring her back and pay if she really turns out guilty? We know darn well she's not. If she was married and Filson didn't think that he could get away with harassing her anymore, wouldn't that work?"

After thinking about it, the Sheriff nodded his head. "I think that would work. Have her bring her young man in early. We'll have them get married before it ever gets light and you can be gone before Filson hauls his lazy butt out of bed in the morning. Barring any solid evidence showing up between now and then, it should get him off her back and mine."

Mose said, "We'll do. We'll see you early." He pushed John and Trace out the door before they could reveal the fact that none of them thought there was a betrothed anywhere near.

They walked their horses down the main street of the town in silence for several moments, and then finally John asked the obvious question, "So, who's she going to marry?"

Trace gave a humorless laugh. "Forget that. Who's going to approach her?"

"This was Mose's idea. You marrying her, Mose?" John looked over at him in the dark.

Mose's deep chuckle sounded in the awkward pause. "Me? I'm the only one that's for sure not getting married. But think about it. She may love this idea. This might be the best thing that could happen to her if he's been bothering her. If it was understood that it would just be annulled when we get them to the valley of the Great Salt Lake, she might be thrilled that Trace is willing to give up bachelorhood for her."

"Me? Why me? Mose Brown, I am *not* bracing her with this idea. She might love it and she might just be thoroughly insulted."

John weighed in. "Mose is right, Trace. You're the only one that I could support this idea with. There's no one else that I'd trust to do it other than Mose here, and mixed race marriage is not all that popular in this state. You're the man."

Trace groaned. "So... What's plan B?"

Mose asked. "How bad do you want to leave? And what's the problem anyway? You told me you almost asked her to marry you on the spot the first time you saw her. Now's your chance."

"You're not all that funny, Mose. We're in a fix here. Be serious."

In a sober tone Mose said, "I'm being plumb serious. I'll approach her, but it will make you look like you're afraid."

Trace gave a small laugh in the dark. "I am afraid. Terrified! Both of her and of marriage." After a moment he relented. "I'll approach her. But you two owe me. You owe me fierce. I'm going to be spending the whole trip across thinking about what I want from you, so be ready, 'cause it's going to be whoppin'."

John sounded relieved. "Good. So do we ask tonight? Or wait until mornin'?"

"Tonight. I'm not waking them all up in the middle of the night to ask a woman that I just met to marry me. Not only that, but they need to be able to be planning whether they're staying or going. We owe them that."

They rode the rest of the way in silence. As they approached the gathered wagons, Mose started humming a wedding march and then peeled off toward their own fire while Trace continued on toward the VanKomen's. He didn't know whether to be thoroughly worried or euphoric about this whole idea. He'd soon find out.

He pulled up and got off his horse and was just about to speak when he heard the sound of a cocking gun. The wagon flap moved and the barrel of a pistol appeared, followed by Giselle's head. When she realized who it was, she dropped the muzzle of the gun and took a deep breath and then whispered with her accent, "Oh, Mr. Grayson, you frightened me. I thought you were Henry Filson. What are you doing?"

That's exactly what he was asking himself just about now. "Uhm, you're not going to believe this, but I've come to see if you would consent to marrying me." He put up a hand. "It's just to be able to get you away in the morning, and we'll have it annulled when we get to your valley. It's either that, or stay here and deal with Filson and a trial, and waste more time getting started west."

She looked totally confused for a minute, and then said, "Just a moment." Her head disappeared back inside the wagon cover and he could hear her whispering quietly to someone and then a bare foot and lower leg appeared through the flaps. He realized she was getting out.

He went forward to help her down and she turned to look at him with big eyes in the darkness. She was wearing a nightgown covered with a long robe and her hair was loose and hanging around her shoulders. She was even prettier than when she'd been all dolled up and he questioned again to himself what in the world he was doing, while he waited there to see if she was going to laugh or cuss at him.

He was completely amazed when she looked up at him in wonder and asked in a soft, sweetly Dutch voice, "You'd do that for me? Really?"

He didn't know what to say to that. He'd never experienced anything in his life that would help him figure out what to do in this situation. Finally, he just said, "Uh, yes. I would. But honestly, it's not being totally unselfish. Without you and your grandparents, we can't leave either until we find someone else to take your place. The army won't let trains of less than twenty wagons start out."

He paused for a minute and then decided that being absolutely forthright was in both of their best interests. "I give you my word to be a gentleman. I wouldn't expect anything other than your help in getting underway. You needn't worry."

She laughed a sweet laugh at him in the dark and said with her intriguing accent, "Worry? You have just taken a huge load of worry off of me! I don't doubt that I can trust you. I knew that the moment I saw you on the hotel boardwalk. And I fully intend to help all the way across this great journey. I will be glad to. I am more grateful to you than I can say right now. I would love to marry you to get started in the morning. I would be thrilled!"

For a second, he thought she was going to come right up and hug him. Just when he felt relieved that she didn't, she actually did. Just as quickly, she pulled back and looked up at him with a sober face. "Tell me what you need me to do."

Still a bit shaken, he simply said, "Be ready to go into town a little before sunup. We'll meet with the Sheriff, get married and be back and ready to leave at first light."

All she did was look up at him with those wide eyes and say, "Okay." With that, she turned around and climbed back into her wagon without a backward glance at him. He walked away in the moonlight in a stupor. He got clear back to his wagon before he remembered that he'd left his horse at the VanKomen's, and he had to go back and get it. Gathering his reins, he was turning to go when she poked her head out again.

Feeling a little sheepish, he said, "Sorry. Forgot my horse." After a thought, he turned back around and said, "Miss VanKomen, you can go to sleep and rest easy. My dog will be right here between our wagons and he's an excellent watch dog. If any one was to approach, he'd let us know and we could handle it before anyone could get near your wagon. And all of my men will be alert for trouble too. You can sleep without worrying about Filson."

She took a deep breath and smiled at him. "Thank you, Mr. Grayson. That will help me. Good night."

CHAPTER 2

The next morning, as he felt the sun climb the sky and shine warmly upon his back, Trace was still wondering what had happened. Walking alongside his horse the cavalcade of white-topped wagons strung out along the road after crossing the wide Missouri River, he realized that, although yesterday he had never even met her, today he was married to the beautiful girl from Holland that he had thought so striking on the boardwalk. Granted, it was a marriage in name only, but still, what a turn of events!

The funny thing about it was that, even as unusual as this whole situation had been, in actuality, it hadn't been that earth-shaking of an occurrence. The actual marriage had been as painless as the asking had been. Once he was over the first initial shock of realizing that she was the girl that he'd seen, being with her had turned out to be surprisingly comfortable. Although she had the regal presence of royalty, she had a warm and sweet personality that put him right at ease and made friendship come incredibly easy.

She didn't act like she was terribly familiar with any of this life, but she had a quirky sense of humor that let her laugh at herself and made those around her laugh with her. Already, his men were eating out of her hand and Mose appeared to think she was a cute little sister or something. Crossing the wilderness like this was always a huge undertaking, but this trip was looking more like a huge adventure by the minute.

When Giselle had looked up the boardwalk there in St. Joseph and seen the handsome young man with the long legs and gentle eyes, she had had no idea that she would be married to him within the next fifteen hours. They had come an unbelievably long way in less than a day, but she was incredibly grateful. For the first time in months, she felt safe. She'd known she would be safe with him the moment she'd realized that they would be traveling together, and his brother Mose and even the rest of the men that were beside him were a huge comfort.

Traveling with them was one thing. Now that she was actually married to him, her relief was almost overwhelming. She knew to the center of her heart that there was no way that he would let Filson near her. The very second that she had seen them together she knew that. His utter disdain for the sneaky and mean Missourian had been obvious. Even though their marriage was in name only, she knew that he would protect her, and although she was in a terrible fix, somehow, she knew now that everything would be okay.

Riding along on the wagon seat beside her grandfather, she wondered if she should have told Trace before she had let him marry her that she was two and a half months with child as a result of being attacked by Mormon hating mobbers near St. Louis. Henry Filson had been the ring leader of the group. He'd hounded her for months, both before and after the attack, and seeing him there in St. Joseph last night had been the most discouraging thing imaginable. She'd so hoped that she had seen the last of him when they'd finally left the St. Louis area for good.

Before leaving for the West with the first wagon train of Mormons fleeing the persecution of Missouri and Illinois, Brigham Young had asked her grandfather to do his best to try and obtain payment for the properties that the Saints had to walk away from there. Giselle's grandmother Petja had never actually joined the Church, and she had continued to attend other churches in the area. Josiah had accompanied her every week. Because of this, even though Josiah had been baptized a Mormon, some of the folks that would have nothing to do with the other Mormons had been willing to do business with Josiah.

For more than eighteen months Josiah had worked to receive payment for the homes and farms; ultimately he decided that he'd done all that was possible and taken his wife and granddaughter and finally headed for that illusive Zion in the West. The money he was carrying for Brigham Young and the Saints was concealed in a hidden compartment in the bottom of the wagon, and only he and Petja and Giselle knew anything about it.

Now, married to an obviously capable and respected man, she actually believed that she might be free of Henry Filson. Free except for the child that she carried inside her.

For a time after the attack, she had struggled to come to terms with the fact of becoming pregnant from such a horrible experience and horrible men, but she had finally made her peace with the idea. The part of her that was fair-minded to the core had eventually gotten past the ugliness of it all and focused on the fact that this child was simply an innocent victim like herself. She had vowed to do her best to mother it and protect it from the troubles it would encounter in its life as a result of the circumstances of its conception-through no fault of its own-as well as she could. She still wasn't happy about it, but she was learning to at least not hate what had happened. In her heart, she worried that there were actually two babies. Twins were common in her family, and several times she had dreamed of two babies. She sincerely hoped she was wrong. One baby born into this circumstance would be sad enough.

Looking up at her grandfather's profile, she thought back on all the events that had led them to this place at this time. He and her grandmother had been willing to give up all the ties they had to their families and leave their beloved Holland to come with her to America and join the Saints here. How grateful she was to them for that.

Her parents had at first been horrified and then angry enough to completely disown her when she had announced her intention of joining the Church after being taught by the missionaries she had met on a trip to England. Being shunned

21

from her family had been the most heart-breaking thing she had ever experienced in all of her fifteen years, but she had known that what the missionaries had taught her was true and right and she couldn't deny it. So she had prepared to leave her comfortable life as the daughter of a diplomat of state to make the long trip to be with the other Saints by herself.

Her parents had enlisted her grandparents to talk some sense into her about joining this strange new "cult" church that espoused visions and prophets, and the result of their investigation had been the announcement that her grandfather believed also and he and her grandmother would be leaving for America with her.

It had been a long and troubled road so far, but she knew what she knew and had to make whatever sacrifices she had to to follow the Prophets that she knew to be the servants of God Himself. Sometimes she didn't understand why God had let the terrible things happen to the Saints that had come to pass, but she always trusted that He knew better than she and that she was doing the right things in spite of all the troubles. When the bulk of the Saints had set out west, she had at first thought that things here in Missouri and in Illinois would settle down, but the child that she now carried was proof of just how wrong that idea had been. The mobs and persecution had continued and, in fact, were far worse for some than they had been for Giselle because there were many who didn't really consider the VanKomens Mormons because of her grandmother's refusal to join.

Wondering again if she should have told Trace about all of this, she reminded herself that this marriage had simply been a means to be able to leave the States quickly, and that once safely in the valley of the Great Salt Lake, would be annulled; Trace would be far away in California by the time she delivered. There had been no time for telling anyway. The entire scope of their acquaintance consisted of probably less than an hour of actual time spent together.

A working marital relationship that included complete disclosure wasn't really part of this arrangement, so her

22

conscience was soothed. At any rate, the last thing she wanted to see in Trace's eyes was pity or revulsion because of what had happened. It was better that she say nothing and do all that she could to facilitate as smooth and swift a trip as possible to reach their destinations ahead of Old Man Winter. The inevitable signs of an advancing pregnancy would tell him in time anyway. She couldn't help the situation that she was in. All that she could do was make the best of it as gracefully and cheerfully as possible, which was what she fully intended to do.

That first day of the trip was a strange combination of being unable to do much while they were actually en route, and then scrambling to accomplish all the necessary tasks of life once the train stopped for the night. She and Petja cooked as quickly as possible while the men saw to the task of caring for the teams and securing the stock within the circle of the wagons. Her grandmother had had the foresight to plan ahead for a quick meal, knowing what a long day this would be, and both Trace and Mose appeared pleasantly surprised when Giselle brought them supper just as they were beginning to start making their own. Trace looked up and said, "Thank you, but you didn't need to do this. We can make our own food. We always have."

She shook her head and said, "Mr. Grayson, this is the least we could do after you helped me get away from Henry Filson. And in reality, it is wisest. It takes only a little more time when we are already cooking, and you have responsibilities that need you elsewhere. It makes sense."

He thought about that and then replied, "Miss VanKomen, er Mrs... Giselle, we don't expect you to fix our meals. That wasn't part of this arrangement."

"No, but even though this marriage is in name only, working together to get to the West is good. We should help each other and make this journey with as little trouble as we can. All of us must do whatever we can to hurry. Swiftness could save many problems in the mountains later."

He seemed to know she was right, but wasn't very willing to give in. "We'll see how things go. If you do cook for us, we have to contribute supplies. Otherwise, no deal."

She nodded. "That is fair. And there may be days when things go badly. We will see as you say."

The food was surprisingly good, considering the short amount of time that they had taken to prepare it. And the help had been appreciated. There had been a number of snags to be dealt with when they had put all of the stock together for the first time. The animals had to establish a pecking order and then there were horses and mules and even the VanKomen's milk cow and calf.

Josiah had a mule that was proving to be a hassle. It had tried to kick him as he was harnessing up that morning and now, in with the others, it was acting vicious and running the other stock, especially the cow and calf. Trace always kept his saddle horse staked out near him and thought that maybe staking either the one mule or the cattle would be in order in the future. All they needed was a stupid mule to chase off all their stock.

All day he'd been wondering if they had seen the last of Filson. Knowing the man, he expected him to show up any time-and he did shortly after they had finished dinner. Mose had been expecting trouble as well. Upon hearing the horse, both of them went to find Giselle.

They found her before Filson did, and were both there in front of her when the shifty, overbearing Missourian appeared. Before he even had the chance to address her, Trace tore into him. "What are you doing in my camp, Filson? You're not welcome here. Turn that horse around and crawl back into whatever hole you came out of. You don't have the Sheriff out here to keep me from shooting a hole into your sneaky hide."

The big Missourian didn't back right down like he should have. "That blamed Sher'f wouldn't see that justice was served, so I came to do it on my ownst. Gimme the girl, Grayson. She's a crim'nal, and she ain't going nowheres until I get my two hunnert back and she's punished proper."

Several more of Trace's drivers materialized, as well as John Sykes. Trace's blood began to boil. Generally slow to rile, the thought of this stupid brute demanding Giselle made the ancient warrior's berserk side of him surface with a passion. "The girl is my wife, Filson! And she's going nowhere with a dog like you! Fork your horse and leave. I won't say it again." He reached down and very obviously slipped the leather thong off of the gun on his hip.

Filson swallowed and looked from Trace to Mose and then the men around them. "I'll git, but this aint the end o' this. I'll have my justice. You wait 'n see."

"You're wrong, Filson! This is the end of this! If I see you anywhere near her again, I'll assume that you mean my wife harm and shoot on sight. You and I both know that Sheriff Toblin would know exactly what had happened if your body showed back up in town tied to your horse's saddle. He'd know that you got what you deserved. Don't tempt me, Filson. I've been wishing for a chance at you for years now. Save your sorry carcass and go back to cheating people in St. Louis."

Filson glared at him, but turned his horse and left. Trace and Mose immediately went after their horses, followed by John and the others. As Trace rode out, he looked up to see Giselle watching him with big eyes. "Don't worry, he'll go. We just want to make good and sure. We'll be back." He turned to his dog and said, "Dog, stay." He pointed to Giselle and the huge, grizzled, gray shepherd walked over to her and turned back to look at him. "Good boy, stay." With that, he spun his horse and headed out into the dark with a small cavalcade of men in his wake.

As he rode, he tried to calm the anger that had risen in him so fast. That was a side of him that was completely at odds with the physician in him. The physician in him wanted to heal the human body. This warrior side of him wanted to destroy one human body in particular.

He thought back to the night he had talked to his father of these things before leaving Georgia for good. His father had spoken of good men standing for something and he had been right. It was important for honorable men to be strong. Much as he disliked the anger, it was good to feel passionate in order to protect those less able to protect themselves. Nothing had ever felt as right as protecting Giselle just now. They rode on into the night, knowing that it was men like Filson that must be defeated in order for decent society to flourish. They drove him several miles back down the road toward St. Joe before turning for camp.

Back at the wagons, the anger long gone, he did a few odds and ends and then began to spread his bedroll under the wagon that he had been driving. It was pitch black out, so at first he didn't see Giselle until she was right there with her bedroll, spreading it next to his.

Wondering what in the world was going on, he finally asked her in a whisper, "What are you doing?"

She turned to him and acted like she was surprised that he asked, when she whispered back with her sweet accent, "I am getting ready for bed."

He tried to keep his voice calm when he asked, "Here? With me?"

Continuing to spread things out, she quietly asked, "Where would you like me to sleep, Trace?"

He was a little confused at that. "I thought you would be sleeping in the wagon with your grandmother."

She whispered back again. "All of their things are in the wagon now. There's not room now to sleep there. And my grandparents have been married for almost forty years. They've never slept apart. The last few days in the wagon I've been... How is it said? A fifth wheel? Is there a problem with me sleeping here? I promise not to bother you."

He shook his head hesitantly. "No... It's not a problem. I'm just surprised. But you're welcome. Are you sure you wouldn't be more comfortable with more privacy? Mose could come sleep here with me if you wanted a wagon to yourself."

She sat down on her bedding and looked at him. "Trace, if you don't want me here, I will go, but truly, I would be afraid to sleep by myself under a wagon. I've never slept outside before in my life. And you're my only option unless I sleep near my grandparents' wagon, but then I would have to sleep beside the wagon instead of under it. Tonight that would be okay, but when it rains I would have to find someplace else anyway. I thought, since you're the one that I'm married to, you would be the best choice. No?"

It all sounded perfectly logical. He just couldn't imagine actually being able to sleep with such a beautiful girl this close to him. Still, he had no idea how to tell her that. "No, you're right. You'd be better here than anywhere else. And I don't mind if you do. Do you have everything that you need?"

She started taking her hair out of the braid that wound around her head. "Yes, I think I am fine, thank you. Good night." She shook out her hair, knelt to pray, and then took off the robe that she was wearing over her nightgown and climbed under the covers. Turning on her stomach, she sighed and then said in a tired voice, "Thank you, Trace. For everything. It has been a long day."

Trace put both hands under his head and looked up at the black bottom of the wagon above him in the dark. Under the next wagon over he heard Mose begin to chuckle and then stifle it with a cough. Oh brother! How was he ever going to live this down? Or sleep? Her lying there beside him was about the most unbelievable turn of events of all. His whole life had been turned upside down in one day.

But then married people did sleep beside each other. Even though this wasn't really a normal marriage, maybe this arrangement wasn't all that strange. He sighed and tried to figure out what he would have been thinking about if she hadn't shown up here. His brain wasn't even functioning and he couldn't think very well. A few minutes later, he was amazed to realize that she was asleep already.

Apparently this wasn't that big of a deal to her. She didn't appear at all uptight about it. Either that or she hadn't slept much the night before. She hadn't appeared tired at dinner, but then he'd never seen her at a dinner before to know what she looked like tired.

With thought after thought tumbling around in his mind, at length the strenuous day took its toll and he drifted off. Only once in the night-when she turned in her sleep and her head was close enough to him that he could smell flowers-did he wake up and realize again that a beautiful girl slept next to him. This time, he was tired enough to simply think it was kind of nice before he went back to sleep.

Waking in the cool darkness before the sun came up, he lay there for a minute wondering about the dream he had had...that she was sleeping next to him... and then she moved in her sleep and he sat up so fast that he whacked his head on the wagon bottom above. In a rush it came back to him, and he looked in wonder over at her there in the dark. Jehosaphat! It was real. He hadn't dreamed last night.

She was beautiful asleep. Both the regal bearing and the sweet sense of humor were gone and there was only the raw beauty and simple vulnerability that emanated from her. Some innate sense that was the remnant of the primitive male within him made a need to take care of and protect her rise in him like hunger or thirst would. It was a basic, primal instinct that was as vital as the need for air. He looked at her for another moment and then got up. He had to get busy or he was never going to make it all the way across this land with her. Already, she was mixing up his head.

He went through his morning's tasks in record time, and when he came back with a pair of mules twenty minutes later, he was surprised to see that her bed was gone and there was no sign that she had ever been there to muddle his brain like she had. He turned to find her bending over the fire stirring something in a pot, her hair neatly braided around her head again and dressed and ready for the day.

Not only was she ready to go, but his breakfast was too. On approaching her at the fire, she handed him a bowl of corn mush and a plate of eggs and bacon, and said, "We haf already ask a blessing over it." He'd noticed the cage of chickens that was strapped to the back of their wagon, but he'd never had an egg while out on the trail. The tall glass of milk that she offered was the final treat. He dug into his breakfast with relish. Maybe this marriage thing was going to be great!

Trace automatically started out in the lead of the train with the VanKomen wagon next and then Mose's, followed by their other drivers. They established an unspoken system of protecting her between them. It was doubtful that Filson would approach the train in broad daylight, but just in case, they would be ready. At any rate, there would be a buffer zone between Josiah and his family and the other, rougher element that followed in the rear of the train.

That day passed quickly, although the infernal dust had already begun to boil up around the wheels of the wagons. Being at the front helped, but it was an early reminder of the misery that this trail could inflict. They paused at midday and ate the lunch that the women had packed and let the stock graze for a few minutes before heading out again. The midsummer weather, albeit hot, was good for making progress and they pushed on steadily.

That evening, Trace helped Josiah stake out the troublesome mule and things went better with the stock. Dinner was ready for them once again when they were through with the animal chores, and Trace thought again that he could get used to this in a hurry. He was sitting by Mose as he ate and he wondered when Mose was going to say something to him about last night's sleeping arrangements. They'd hardly spoken all day through the long pull, but he expected something now that they were seated and had a moment. He knew Mose too well to think that he was going to let last night pass without some kind of ribbing.

Actually, when it came, there wasn't much tease to it. Mose just looked at him with a grin and asked, "Ja get any sleep last night? After your company arrived?"

Trace grinned back. "I did, actually. Well, after a while." He paused as they ate. "Never dreamed she'd do that, but it wasn't too bad."

Mose looked off into the distance, and the grin died out of his face. At length he said quietly, "Sleeping beside Callie was the greatest peace I've ever known."

Trace didn't answer that. In the first place, he didn't understand. Last night was the only time in his life that he'd slept anywhere near a woman. And in the second place, what could you say to a friend that had watched his wife die so tragically? He knew that, even after more then three years, Mose mourned.

His smile had finally come back, although it had taken a while, but there were still times he knew that he was thinking about her. Trace had never had a woman he cared about the way that Mose had adored Callie. He'd have almost thought it was weird except that his parents loved each other that way. In a way he was a little jealous of his friend even though Mose had lost his love. It must be nice to have a friendship like that with your wife.

The two of them sat there like that for a while. In spite of the differences in color, or perhaps because of it, there had never been two closer friends. They considered each other a brother, but what they had went far beyond mere brotherhood. There were times that they read each other's minds. Lots of times. That uncanny link had been the catalyst to many a good business deal, and more than once, it had saved each of their hides.

As they quietly sat there, Giselle came and took her bedroll out of the wagon and set it back under Trace's and then disappeared for a moment. She reappeared and rolled the bedding out and then did the same thing she had the night before: shook out her hair, said her prayers, and took off her robe to lie down. She appeared to go to sleep within minutes again and Trace wondered at her ability to drop off so quickly under new and strange circumstances. He knew she had worked hard and for long hours these last two days, but after her admission that she had never slept outside, he'd expected some little period of adjustment.

A few minutes later, Mose got up and gave Trace a wide grin and said "Nighty night" before heading off to his own blankets.

Trace hesitated for a few minutes until he realized that he was doing it. When he admitted to himself that he was a little tentative about going over to sleep beside her, he shook himself. Men the world over would trade him places in a heartbeat. What was he worried about? He was married to her for heaven's sake.

All of his life he'd dreamed of someday finding a beautiful, sweet girl to play house with. So they weren't necessarily playing house, at the very least he could enjoy being by her. So far she'd been really great. He got his bedroll and spread it out beside her, being careful not to wake her. She was as pretty tonight as she'd been this morning, and he lay down next to her with a sigh.

It was good that he was tired to the bone. As he closed his eyes, he was inordinately pleased that Henry Filson hadn't shown up again tonight.

Sometime deep in the night, when Dog growled, he realized that he'd had that thought too soon. He reached next to his head and grasped his revolver, the sound of the hammer cocking back loud in the still night. Giselle opened her eyes and looked at him. Silently he mouthed for quiet and went to get up, but Mose's voice sounded out before he moved.

It was almost conversational. "Trace, you know that galoot that you threatened to shoot on sight a couple nights ago? I've got him here by the throat. You want me to just throttle him or you want to come out here and shoot him as promised?"

Trace smiled at Giselle to calm the fear that he saw in her eyes and sat up to put his boots on. He answered in the same conversational tone. "Save him for me to shoot. There are those that would come after you for wringing a white's neck. I'll be right there. Take him out to the edge of the flat. I don't want to get blood on any of our gear."

He got up and shrugged into his shirt and strapped on his gun belt and walked toward the sound of Mose's voice. What to do with this fool? He ought to shoot him, but the physician side of him would rail at that unless he had no choice. So then, what? What would make this slob yearn for a different clime?

Approaching Mose, one of the others arrived as well, leading a saddled horse. Mose truly did have the guy by the throat and he was all but blue when Trace encouraged him to let go. Trace nonchalantly began to unsaddle the horse and said over his shoulder to Filson, "Start shucking those clothes, you piece of coyote bait. I'm going to make you wish I'd shot you long before I actually do it."

Still gasping for breath, Filson whined, "What do you mean?"

Turning from the horse, Trace grasped the front of the heavy Missourian's shirt and literally jerked it off of him. "I said exactly what I mean. Take 'em off. All of 'em. Right down to your dirty, fat hide. Now!"

Filson's eyes looked more frightened than ever and Trace said, "All I'm going to do is make you ride this razorback of yours the thirty something miles back to St. Joe without the comfort of any padding. I'm going to give you a running start before I start shooting. It might be thirty yards, it might be a hundred. You never know.

"You'll just know that you're gonna be riding for your life and hope you make it out of range before I hit your big, gleaming, white backside. But this is the last time I'm gonna give you a break. Next time, I truly will be aiming for your heart, and I'm a good shot."

By this time, there were nine men standing together in the dark and one of them asked, "Trace, you gonna hog all that shootin' to yourself? Or can any of us take a crack at his glowing hiney?"

Trace turned. "Y'all boys want in?" Several of them answered in various styles to the affirmative and Trace smiled. "There's not going to be any prize for whoever gets the best shot. Other than knowing that you've done all of Missouri a favor. You're sure?" More interesting yeses followed and Trace said, "All right, but let him get out there a ways. No sense in spoiling the sport o' the deal."

He turned to Filson who actually was almost glowing in the moonlight, naked as he was. "Get on up there, man. Before one of these boys goes to jumping the gun, so to speak." After several ridiculously ungainly tries, Filson finally made it onto the ribby steed, at which point Trace calmly reached and took the bridle off. "Good luck, Filson, you're gonna need it." He gave the horse a resounding slap on the rump and it took off on a lunging run with Filson bouncing and scrambling to hang on.

When he was forty yards out, Trace raised his gun, and to a man, the others followed suit. At his word they all let loose and the fleeing rider kicked the horse up to a frantic pace. After an ongoing volley of shots, the pale bouncing figure disappeared into the night and the remaining teamsters headed back to camp, laughing and slapping each other on the back as they went.

Mose shook his head and chuckled. "One day you're gonna have to quit fooling around and shoot him, Trace. Much as you hate the idea. Your little wife truly isn't safe until you do."

Trace sighed. "I know. Actually, I was hoping that one of those boys didn't know me well enough to know that I was just scaring him. But I think he got away. Next time."

Mose threw a big arm around his shoulder. "Think positive. Maybe one of us at least winged him."

"Winged or not, he's not going to want to ride a horse for a while. Maybe we'll have a day or two to get further out."

"Probably not, but we can hope. We should get back. Your little Dutch girl thinks that you just had a man shot to ribbons in her behalf. You got some 'splainin' to do, son."

Trace elbowed him. "Quit pretending to not be able to speak correctly. You did better in school than I did. And I'm a doctor. Son."

Mose elbowed him back. "Yes, Massa." At that point Trace tackled him in the grass, and within about a minute, Mose had him tied in a knot and then laughed, "Quit horsing around. Giselle is going to be upset." He stood up and offered Trace a big hand.

They walked into camp and went their separate ways. Trace ducked under the wagon and started to take off his boots. Giselle was lying there, big-eyed, and he lay down with a sigh and then turned and leaned on an elbow to tell her what happened. "We didn't really shoot him. We never intended to, but he didn't know that." She breathed a huge sigh of relief.

Looking at her steadily, he continued, "But I'm going to have to if he comes again, Giselle. And I think that he will." She nodded silently. Trace rolled back over muttering. "Stupid idiot. I'm a doctor not a gunfighter, but at some point I have to make a stand. I probably already should have done it."

She put a gentle hand on his arm. "I'm sorry to have brought you so much trouble, Trace. If he comes again, I will shoot him myself. That is too much to ask another to do. But remember that God feels it is okay to take a life in defense of life and liberty. It is better that one man perish, remember?" She was right and he knew it. It just went against the grain to spend part of his time trying to heal people and then turn around and shoot someone.

He was almost back to sleep when she asked, "What did you mean you're a doctor not a gunfighter?"

He yawned and replied, "Nothing, Elle. I just don't like killing. Ruins my whole day. Ya' know?"

"I would imagine so." She sounded more asleep than awake. "Thank you again, Trace. Good night."

CHAPTER 3

Within just a few days the train had fallen into a routine. The stock settled into the pull and the people learned to work together to get the cavalcade on down the trail. Giselle seemed to be getting used to the journey, and the milking that had obviously been exhausting when she first started appeared to have become much easier over the past days. Houses and farms became more scarce, and it wasn't long before civilization was left further and further behind.

Five days out, in the middle of the night, Dog growled again. Trace reached for his gun and glanced over at Giselle's bed before he cocked it. Her bed was empty, and his breath caught. *Had Filson made it into camp and gotten away with her without anyone even knowing?* Trace took the gun and ghosted into the night toward the sound of the dog growling. Mose was gone from his bed as well, and Trace suspected that Filson had already been apprehended. His big friend was like an Indian at times. He could move through the dark with no more sound than a ghost.

Without yet having located Filson or Mose, Trace realized that Giselle was sitting in the brush in front of him with a rifle raised to her shoulder and rested on her upturned knee. Before he had a chance to get to her, the big gun went off, the concussion shattering the silence of the night. She quietly lowered the gun and slipped back into the darkness, and though he tried to follow, he couldn't see which way she went.

Trace heard sounds and carefully headed that way, his gun in his hand. Ahead of him, someone struck a light and he moved towards it, afraid of what he might find. Two of his teamsters were standing over a figure on the ground while Mose walked toward him from the other side of them. The four men stood and looked down at the body of Filson as he lay there in an ugly, black circle of blood. None of them bothered to check for signs of life. If he wasn't dead, he soon would be.

The two drivers looked up and one of them asked, "Who shot him?" Mose glanced over and met Trace's eyes and he knew that Mose also knew as well that it was Giselle.

Mose answered, "I was still trying to sneak up on him when I heard the shot. Was it you, Trace?"

Trace nodded in the affirmative, without saying anything, and Mose asked, "Do we bury him? Or send him back on his horse?"

With a sigh, Trace said, "Let's bury him. No sense in borrowing trouble. Help me lift him would you, Mose?"

Shaking his head, Mose looked at him. "I'll handle burying him. These boys will help me. You'd better get on back to camp and see to things there."

Trace glanced up. "Thanks, man." He headed back towards his wagon, wondering where Giselle had gone in the dark. Still a ways away, he heard something out in the brush and turned toward the sound. He found her on her knees being violently sick with the gun beside her. Speaking low, he came up to her and put a hand gently on the small of her back and left it there while she finished retching. Wordlessly, he handed her a handkerchief to wipe her face and mouth.

She didn't look up, just said, "Thank you," and then picked up the gun and turned to head back.

He reached and caught her arm and looked down into her face. For a second or two he studied her in the dark and then asked, "You okay?" She nodded, but tears welled up in her eyes and began to stream down her cheeks. Pulling her into a gentle hug, he rubbed her shoulder while she cried like her heart was broken. At length he said sadly, "I wish you wouldn't have done that. It's going to be hard to deal with. I know from experience."

She shook her head against his chest. "I had to." After a pause she took a deep breath and continued. "I couldn't put anyone else in danger anymore and that's too much to expect another to do for me. He was my problem. I wish he could have been removed long ago. It would have saved a lot of heartache." She continued to cry quietly and then added, "He was a very bad person that didn't care who he hurt. He would never have left me alone until he was forced to." She sniffled and wiped her eyes with the back of her hand.

Still holding her, he asked, "How long has he been bothering you?"

"He first saw me more than a year ago. For a while he just tried to pay attention to me. Then he got more demanding. The last few months have been horrible. I couldn't do that to all of you. He wouldn't care who he hurt to get to me. He had to be stopped."

He pulled back and raised her face to look at him. "It's still going to be awful to get over, but you're right. He did have to be stopped. I don't believe there was any other way he could have been handled. It was what I fully intended to do when I found him tonight. It was in defense of that life and liberty that you spoke of. Remember that." She hid her face in his chest and began to cry again.

At length she raised her head and asked, "Do they all know that I did it?"

"Just Mose. We let the others think it was me."

She shook her head again. "I can't let you take the blame for me. If the Sheriff comes you would be in trouble."

This time, he shook his head. "The Sheriff isn't going to come. There's no such thing as a Sheriff out here. I'm fine with taking the blame. I'd rather than that they thought it was you. Do you want your grandparents to know?"

"Of course not, but I should be honest. You shouldn't be blamed for something so terrible that you didn't do."

"Giselle, look at me. There are some that would say that what you have done is a service to society. You yourself know that to be true or you wouldn't have done it. Let's just let this lie as it is. If there's ever a problem, we'll tell everyone the truth then. How does that sound?"

For several seconds, she looked up into his eyes and finally nodded. "Good. I think it's best this way. Do you think that you can come back to bed yet?" She nodded wordlessly again and he reached down to take the gun for her and then waited while she went on ahead of him.

Camp was dark and quiet when they made their way back to their beds. He lay down, but she knelt to pray. He knew that she had started to cry again as she prayed, and when she lay down and curled into a ball facing away from him, he leaned up on an elbow to whisper, "Giselle, is there any way that you could not turn away from me right now?"

She rolled over and faced him with her tear filled eyes. "What?"

Gently, he said. "Don't try to face this by yourself tonight, Elle. At least let me be your friend through it. It's hard enough, without feeling like you're alone." She nodded and he reached for her hand. "Pray for peace, Elle. I'll pray for you too. And I'm sure Mose is praying as well. It might be a long night, but we'll get through it."

She turned on her side and moved her head over next to his shoulder. "Thanks, Trace. For everything. I'm sorry for the trouble. Good night."

"You're welcome. And the trouble's okay. That particular one is over anyway." He squeezed her hand. "Good night, Elle."

Once in the night he heard her crying again and rolled over and put his arm across her. When he awoke in the last dark before dawn, he was surprised to see Dog curled up beside her. Dog actually had his head on her arm and Trace wondered if he had known that she was deeply sad somehow. He must have, because he was fairly haunting her as she cooked when Trace came back through a few minutes later.

Her bedroll still lay beside his under the wagon and he quickly rolled them both up and tossed them inside his wagon before coming to the fire. He stopped beside her and she looked up at him steadily. She looked like she'd been upset, but she was going to be okay. He could see that in the resolute expression in her eyes. He dropped a hand to her shoulder and gave it a squeeze as she handed him a plate and cup. "Thanks, Giselle. It looks and smells wonderful."

Giselle didn't think it smelled wonderful. After having thrown up in the night, this morning her stomach was roiling. It had been this way off and on during this pregnancy, but never as bad as it was this morning. She got breakfast ready, but after handing Trace his, she had to hurry to get out of camp before she was sick again in the brush beside the nearby stream. When she was finished, she was embarrassed to see that Mose was not far away and had seen how sick she was. He came to her and gently asked, "You okay?"

Nodding, she said, "I'm fine," and hurried back toward camp. That morning after chores were done, and they pulled out, she talked to her grandparents for a while on the wagon seat as they drove. Josiah asked about the shooting the night before, and she told him that Filson had been killed and left it at that. Just thinking about it made her nauseous again and she had to climb down from the wagon and run to be sick. She knew Mose had seen it again, but there was nothing she could do about that.

Once back aboard, she felt awful and her grandmother encouraged her to climb into the back and try to find a place to rest as they traveled. Giselle gladly took her up on her offer. She was still there when they stopped for lunch and her grandmother brought her some food, hoping it would be easier to keep down while the wagon was still for a few minutes. Both Trace and Mose looked in on her, which made her feel both better and worse. It was great to be taken such good care of, but she so regretted bringing trouble into their train.

The afternoon went a little better, and by the time they stopped to circle into camp, she was able to face cooking again. She ate a minimal dinner, finished the chores of cleaning up and milking, and then went to bed immediately after praying to do better the next day.

After gratefully sleeping through an uneventful night, the next day did go better. She was sick again very first thing, but then was able to make breakfast, do the milking, and pack their lunch without having to run back out of camp again. She slept part of the afternoon in the back of the wagon too and that helped. This baby-or babies-made her so tired that she could hardly fathom it. That evening her grandmother did most of the cooking, but Giselle was able to get the other chores done and, after eating, went straight back to bed. She was sleeping so hard that she didn't even know if Trace came to sleep by her because he was up and gone when she dragged out of bed the next morning.

Once more sick to the core, she rushed out of camp to be ill. Afterwards, she sat on a big flat rock on the way back to rest for just a second. She pulled her legs up beside her and bowed her head, knowing that she needed some help to get the terrible nausea under control. She needed to feel better than this to be able to handle all that this trip to Zion required of her, and no matter what, she didn't want to become a burden that would slow them down. She heard a sound and opened her eyes to see Mose looking at her from across the little clearing.

She quickly got up and began to walk back to camp, but had to stop again before she made it very far. She had already lost what little was in her stomach this morning, so why was she still so green? Being caught by Mose again made her a little embarrassed around him later when she handed him his breakfast.

Finally, this day went better than the last couple and she felt so much stronger that she hoped that she could put the worst of the morning sickness behind her again and get back to focusing on what needed to be done. That evening after dinner and the regular chores, she hurried to heat water in the big kettle to wash some laundry before dropping into bed dead tired again.

Whether it was the laundry or just being with child, the next morning, she was up even before Trace, being ill in the dark as far from camp as she was able to make it before she had to stop. She tried to be completely quiet, but apparently she wasn't quiet enough, because a minute or two later, Mose appeared out of the pre-dawn gray. He walked up to her and handed her a handkerchief and a cold biscuit without saying a word, and then stood there with her while she wiped her mouth and moved to a nearby fallen tree to sit down. She started to eat the biscuit, praying that it would somehow help her feel good enough to make it back to camp and through the morning.

Surprisingly, the biscuit did help. She finished it and then stayed seated for a minute to let it settle before starting back towards the wagons to get breakfast. Mose had just been looking at her this whole time and she wondered what she should say when, out of the blue, he said, "I was married once. Did you know that?" His voice was tired when he said it.

She looked up at him, but it was hard to read his expression in the dim light. "Was? You're not anymore?"

He shook his head and then went on in an incredibly sad voice. "She died."

Giselle didn't know what to say or why he had told her that just now. "I'm so sorry, Mose."

"Me too." He almost whispered it. After a long pause he continued in a more conversational tone, looking her in the face all the while. "She was expecting a baby before she died. She was sick just like this." He gestured towards her and then waited for her to say something.

She looked up at him again, loathe to speak out loud the devastating truth that so far she'd only shared with her grandparents. She had no idea how to go about telling something so hard to face. Especially not to someone that she hadn't known long. Before she had figured out how to answer him, he came right out and asked, "Where is the father?"

Dropping her eyes, she shook her head and said in a voice as sad as his was, "I was in the wrong place at the wrong time when a mob of Mormon haters came, Mose. I don't even know which one of them was the father. The only one I even knew was Filson. He was the leader."

There was what felt like a long, long pause before he said, "You need to tell Trace. He'd want to know."

She was finally able to look up. "I can't." She hesitated and then shook her head again. "I can't. And there's no need. Eventually, I won't be able to hide it and our marriage will be annulled and you'll both be in California long before it's due anyway. I'm sorry. I can't face Trace just yet. The only ones other than you now that know are my grandparents."

He was more adamant this time. "He'd want to know, Miss Giselle. He really is a doctor. A very good one. He would want to be able to take better care of you. There's a reason they call it a delicate condition. And even though your marriage is a little unusual, you are married."

She shook her head. "Not really, Mose. And that's not the point anyway. Whether it's a delicate condition or not doesn't change what I need to do to help get west as fast as possible. Delay could well mean our lives. All of our lives."

"Miss Giselle, it's none of my business, but there's no reason in the world not to adjust a few things to take better care of you."

She raised her chin. "I'm absolutely fine, just as things are. So I'm sick when I get up and I tire easily. That's nothing I can't handle." She got up. "Let's don't talk about this anymore. It's better if I try not to think about it."

Stopping her, he said, "No, Giselle, even if it was conceived in a horrible situation, a baby is a blessing from God. It was not its fault. And a new life should be celebrated."

"That's easy for you to say, Mose. Sometimes reality isn't everything it should be." She turned to go and then paused and turned back to him. "Mose, where is your baby?"

His face clouded. "The baby died too, Giselle. But it wasn't mine. My wife was a slave. She died trying to deliver her master's child."

Her eyes flew to his. After a few seconds she said in almost wonder, "But you would have celebrated its new life." It wasn't a question.

He hesitated. "I'm no saint, Miss Giselle, but the life of a slave is hard enough. Add to that the stigma of being a mixed race child born in those circumstances. That child would have had enough trouble without being rejected by its own father. And I would have been its father just as Callie would have been its mother. Jesus would have wanted it that way."

She came back to him and stood in front of him to look up. "Thank you, Mose. I needed to hear that."

He shrugged. "Everyone has their own troubles, Miss Giselle. We just have to do the best we can with the hand we're dealt."

They turned to walk side by side back to camp. Before they reached it, she turned to him and asked, "Are you going to tell Trace?"

He shook his head. "That's not my place, Giselle... But he'd want to know."

Hesitating for a few seconds while she thought about that, she finally shook her head. "I can't, Mose. I can't. Not yet."

Walking back into the quiet circle of wagons, she stopped and looked at Trace lying there still asleep. What Jesus would have wanted. That's what Mose had said about celebrating another man's child. What would Jesus have wanted in her situation? Would He want her to tell Trace or protect him from the truth as long as possible? She had no idea. Still wondering, she went to start breakfast, grateful for Mose's biscuit and the help it had been in settling her stomach.

When Trace appeared and she dished him up his food, he stopped and hesitantly asked her, "Have I offended you somehow, Giselle?"

Surprised, she looked up at him. "Not at all, why?"

He shrugged, watching her. "You just haven't spoken to me much the last couple of days. You're already asleep when I come to bed and this morning you were even gone when I got up. I just wondered if you're avoiding me for some reason since that Filson mess the other night."

She faced him and decided to be as honest as she could. "You haven't offended me, Trace. On the contrary, you've been wonderful. The other night made me a little sick to my stomach and it's still rather unpredictable. And I've been tired. But I'll do better about being more myself. I'm sorry that you had to wonder."

Gently, he asked her, "Are you okay? About the other night, I mean?"

Looking down she admitted, "It is better if I can not think about it. That is for sure. But when I do think about it, I always come back to the fact that I knew that I needed to stop him. Looking back, I think I did what I had to do. But life is precious. Even his. And death is very permanent."

He put a hand on her shoulder. "Give it some time. You're going to be fine eventually. I promise."

She put a hand up to his on her shoulder. "I think you're right. Thank you."

She made it a point to be awake when he came to his bed that night, even as tired as she was. The next morning as she was waking, he was already up and gone. She lay there in her bedding, hesitating, because she knew that as soon as she sat up, she was going to be sick. While she was still lying there, Mose came by and handed her another cold biscuit and said, "Eating a little something before she got up always helped my Callie. Maybe this will help you feel better."

Taking it gratefully, she hoped he was right. "Thank you, Mose. I owe you."

"No, Miss Giselle, I'm still clear behind in owing you, but I'm working on it." He smiled and went on about his morning chores, and a few minutes later Giselle got up and went about hers too. The biscuit worked wonderfully and she felt happier and more energetic that day than she'd felt in a long, long time. Every morning after that, Mose would come and slip her a biscuit, and the nausea became much more manageable.

CHAPTER 4

Slowly, but surely, she was learning how to do all the new things she had to do. She had cooked in Holland, but most of the other things like laundry, milking, or even driving the mules were things that she had always had done for her back home. It had been hard to learn to be more self sufficient here in America, and especially here in the wagon train, but her sense of pride and accomplishment were well worth the trouble.

The one thing that she was still having trouble with was learning to knit. One of the sister Saints in Nauvoo had started teaching both her and Petja before leaving on an earlier train, and Petja had become accomplished, but Giselle couldn't seem to get it. She was the first to laugh at herself as she struggled with the long needles and tangles of yarn, and it had become something of a teasing point among the five of them.

So far the hardest thing to deal with was the fact that she was becoming foolishly attached to Trace. Even though she knew that their married days were numbered, and that when they reached the valley of the Great Salt Lake he would be leaving her as fast as he could to get over the mountains, she still thoroughly enjoyed being around him far too much. She was trying not to, but he was a hard man not to be enamored with. Not only was he very good looking, he was also hard-working, generous, smart, and gentle and... The list could go on and on, although Giselle was constantly trying not to notice all of this.

Nights were the hardest. Sometimes she was ridiculously aware of this very attractive man sleeping next to her and sleep was a little elusive. Not only that, but several times when she had

had a bad dream, he would simply put a hand on her shoulder or back, and the fear would miraculously dissipate to be replaced by a sweet peace that she basked in. They weren't far into their journey when she realized that she would be perfectly happy to travel with him like this for however long she could.

They also weren't very far into their journey when the problems that they had known they would encounter along the way became troubling. The dust had been a problem from nearly the first day, but because they were near the front of the wagon train, they had been spared the misery that the men at the back had been enduring. At first Giselle had wondered why the wagons didn't change positions, but then she'd heard the wagon master talking to Trace about the fact that he wanted Trace to lead out and find the best travel routes and water and camp spots.

Everyone in the train deferred to Trace's judgment on most everything, and it made her respect him all the more. However, even with his wonderful judgment, finding enough feed for the stock en route was a problem. The settler trains that had gone before had eaten most of the grass down and crushed what they didn't eat, and this late in the year, there wasn't much new graze growing.

She'd known that people in their own train would be problematic as well, but she didn't know how soon that would occur. Twice Trace and Mose had made reference to Trace being a doctor, but she hadn't truly realized that they were serious until one night when one of the teamsters was brought back to the train with a gunshot wound.

They had passed Fort Kearney that day, and after going into camp that night, some of the more unruly drivers had headed into the fort to go to the saloon that was nearby. Trace and Giselle were already in bed and asleep when they were awakened by the rather inebriated teamsters. Apparently, some of them had had words with men at the fort and an argument had broken out. Shots had been fired and one of the teamsters was in danger of bleeding to death from a bullet wound in his side. Not only was he bleeding, but the bullet was still lodged in him.

Trace immediately got out of bed and Giselle followed, wondering what was going on. They took the unconscious driver and laid him on the tailgate of one of the wagons and put three lanterns next to him. Mose appeared with a black medical bag and Trace washed his hands twice and then proceeded to examine the ugly wound. Giselle was so amazed as she watched him remove the bullet and begin cleaning and stitching the ragged hole that she didn't even think about being sick at the gore. It wasn't until she felt lightheaded as he cleaned and bandaged the now neatly stitched hole that she realized she was going to be violently ill.

This time they all knew that she lost it. She hadn't made it thirty feet away from the area where they were working before she was sick. On returning to bed a while later, Trace looked at her in the dark with concern. "You okay, Elle?"

Embarrassed, she tried to act like it was nothing. "I'm fine. Actually, I thought it was fascinating. You really are a doctor! For some reason, I didn't think you were serious that night. I was so busy being amazed that I didn't realize I was going to be sick. Sorry."

Gently he said, "It's okay. Does blood bother you?"

She shook her head. "Not usually." She paused. "Why are you freighting goods when you are an accomplished physician?"

He sounded a little hesitant in the dark. "I honestly don't know the answer to that. My father is a doctor back in Georgia; and I helped him for years and then went to a medical college in Pennsylvania for two years. I wanted to go another year, but Mose's wife died and it changed some things for us. It was a bad experience.

"My parents didn't have slaves. In fact they adopted Mose right into our family when he was seven. He'd been brought to my father after being beaten into a coma. We weren't slavers, but many of the people there were. His wife was a slave.

"After Callie's death, Mose was so different, and I wanted to get as far away from slavery as I could. I couldn't go back to school and leave Mose just then. He needed me. We'd heard that in the territories Blacks were more accepted, so we came west and tried a few things and I liked being in business for myself. It used to frustrate me when a huge portion of being a doctor was simply repairing the awful things that one human being did to another."

He shrugged. "I've matured or something, because now I deal with that much better. And Mose is okay now. He still misses his wife terribly sometimes, but he's learned how to be happy again.

"I imagine that sometime I'll open an office somewhere and settle down, but first there are more places that I need to see and things I need to try. In the mean time, humans keep getting shot or thrown or broken somehow, so I do a surprising amount of the kind of thing I did tonight to stay tuned up."

She leaned up on an elbow and smiled at him. "I thought you were marvelous! I was so proud of you!" She said several other things with enthusiasm before Trace laughed and put up a hand.

"Whoa, Elle. Whoa! English. Speak English. If I'm going to get compliments, I at least want to know what they are. I don't speak Dutch, darlin'. Pretty good English. A touch of Spanish and some Indian dialects, but my Dutch is abysmal."

She put a hand to her forehead. "Did I switch into Dutch? I am so sorry. Sometimes I do that when I'm excited." She paused and then said more earnestly, "I was just saying that I thought you were wonderful tonight. You have many wonderful gifts. More than your fair share. I was so proud for you." She lay back down, almost a little embarrassed, until he turned on his side and took her hand.

"Thanks, Elle. It's nice to be told that sometimes." He squeezed her hand and then set it down. "We'd better sleep fast. Morning's not far off and it will be a long day."

She sighed a sleepy, happy sigh. "I am tired. Good night, Doctor Grayson."

He chuckled and turned onto his back again. "Good night, Giselle."

It took her a while to get back to sleep that night. The closeness she had felt to him while they talked made sleep elusive. When she did finally drift off, it seemed like only minutes before she felt him wake her by gently rubbing her back. Finally coming awake, she was breathing heavily, and her heart was pounding in fear. In her dream, she'd been runing from the mob again. It was a nightmare that she'd had many times and it brought the horror of that night back with a terrifying intensity.

Almost instinctively, she rolled to him and buried her head against him. He wrapped an arm around her and hugged her close, talking to her gently. After a while, his strength and the comfort of his voice were able to dispel her fear miraculously. Oh, if only she'd have been able to turn to him like this in the past weeks and months when this fear had threatened to swallow her. Relaxing into him, she sighed and let her exhausted body go back to sleep, knowing that no one would hurt her while he was near.

Trace had come wide awake in the night, instantly alert. It took him a second to realize that what had woken him was Giselle lying beside him. She had curled into a ball and was breathing heavily. As he went to put a hand on her shoulder, she cried right out in fear and jerked away. He rolled over on his side and began to rub her back and talk to her to get through the nightmare to her. He could feel her heart racing right through the flannel of her nightgown.

She awakened and lay there for just a second and then rolled over tightly against him and buried her face in his chest. He wrapped his arm around her and pulled her close and just held her and quietly talked to her while her breathing subsided and she calmed down. She never even surfaced for air and he wondered what she would be dreaming about that would frighten her so much. She'd had bad dreams several times while she'd been sleeping here under his wagon beside him, but he'd never seen her this afraid.

He felt her slowly relax against him and eventually she went back to sleep, still without pulling away from his chest. She felt wonderful, snuggled against him, but he was far too aware of having a beautiful girl in his arms in his bed to even think about going to sleep again. For several minutes he felt guilty about thinking this way, but then finally remembered that they really were married and that it was all okay-except for the fact that she thought of him more as a guardian or a brother than a husband. He wanted to pull her even closer and kiss her, but knew that would ruin their friendship and make this whole journey uncomfortable for them both. So he just held her while she slept and did some soul searching about why he no longer wanted to leave her in the valley of the Mormons and go on without her.

He could tell that she wasn't used to this way of life. She'd admitted never having camped out, and she had to learn to do things like milking the cow Josiah had purchased the day before joining them, and driving a team. All but the most privileged in any country would be familiar with tasks like that. She must have come from a very well-to-do family in Holland, but she had set to work alongside the rest of them willingly and with a happy attitude that was very endearing. Her attempts at learning to knit with her grandmother had become the funniest part of this whole journey and had left them all laughing several times in the evenings. Living and working beside her had dispelled some of the image that she was royalty, but only because she was so sweet and funny and down-to-earth when you got close enough to realize it.

Lying here holding her, he wondered why in the world those Mormon men hadn't snatched her right up to marry. They were fools. She was a wonderful girl, not to mention strikingly beautiful. Even camping out for weeks hadn't dulled how exquisite she was.

He never did get back to sleep. There was just no way, and although holding her was hard, in a way, he reveled in it. He held her, marveling in her softness and the way she smelled until it was time to get up. He carefully pushed her aside so that he could move and almost decided to just stay there when she sighed in her sleep and snuggled over to him again. It took all of his self control to get out of bed that morning.

Mose met him where he was starting the campfire a few minutes later and gave him a thorough checking out before saying conversationally, "You look like the wrath of Lucifer this morning. What happened to you?"

Trace chuckled at his brutal bluntness and replied with a sigh, "After the teamster thing, Giselle had a nasty dream. I mean nasty. She was terrified. I woke her up and she spent the rest of the night with her head buried in my chest. It's amazingly hard to rest with a beautiful women glued to you. Did you know that? Not to mention that when you're married, but not really, it kind of tests your self control."

Mose laughed at him, but then said, "I feel for you, Trace. If I'd have had to keep my hands off Callie, I'd have had to move to another state."

"I am moving to another state. Unfortunately she's moving with me. Maybe it's fortunately. As it was, I seriously considered just staying in bed this morning and letting the rest of you move on without us."

This time Mose busted right up with laughter. "I can see you just lying there while the whole rest of the wagon train left without you. What would you have told her when she woke up?"

He grinned. "That I accidentally slept in?"

Shaking his head, Mose laughed again and said, "She's a bit too smart for that. You could always stay married to her, you know."

"I don't think Mormons really marry people who aren't. Plus, I've heard the weirdest things about them."

Mose shrugged his shoulders. "We've been with them for weeks now and all I've noticed is that they work hard, serve each other, never swear and don't go off and get drunk and shoot each other. Seems to me that they have the key to living happily. At least they have a wonderful spirit about them."

Trace considered this. "They really do, don't they? I thought it was just that I was enamored with Giselle, but Josiah and Petja have that same spirit. I hadn't thought of it that way."

Turning to leave, Mose said over his shoulder, "You should start thinking of her that way. She's a good woman. You need her."

As he finished building up the fire for her to cook breakfast, Trace thought about that. Need was too strong a word for this situation, wasn't it? He heard a sound and turned to watch her approaching the fire. No, need was the word all right. She looked positively tempting this morning. Her hair was pulled up and twisted somehow at the back of her head and she looked soft and sweet and still a little sleepy. She looked at him as she came, and walked right up to him to look at him as hard as Mose had. After studying him for a minute she asked, "Are you okay, Trace? You're not sick are you?"

He laughed at that. "No, not sick. Just a little tired."

She dropped her eyes and then looked back up and asked earnestly, "Was it me? Waking you up last night?"

Hesitating, he wasn't sure how to answer that honestly. "Maybe a little. It was probably just those darn teamsters trying to kill themselves at the fort. I'll be fine once I'm awake. Are you okay this morning? You were pretty upset last night. What were you so afraid of? What did you dream?"

Her face clouded and she shook her head. "Just a nightmare. I have it sometimes. I'm sorry that I woke you. Please forgive me." She went to turn aside and begin breakfast, but he stopped her.

"Its okay, Elle. I was glad to help you. It was awful to see you afraid, and being by me did help, didn't it?"

Looking up into his face she said, "Being by you was like heaven when I was that afraid. Thank you. I wish that you would have been there the other times I've dreamed about it. Those times I wasn't able to stop being afraid like last night. You bring me peace. It's a priceless gift. I'm very grateful."

He wanted to touch her but didn't dare. Instead he just said, "You're very welcome." They looked at each other for a second or two and then turned away to get on with their morning chores. All morning she was on his mind.

It was a good thing he had something nice to think about, because the whole morning was a rout. The rowdy teamsters that weren't shot were hung over, and the one that was shot was worthless. At least he was going to live. That was something. It took them an extra hour to get the train headed out that morning, and then within just another couple of hours it began to rain. It settled the dust within seconds, but then it wasn't long before the teams were slogging through mud that thickened by the minute and the drivers were soon miserable in spite of their slickers.

He was on his horse this time, scouting ahead for the best route again and he looked over at Josiah's wagon, glad to see that at least Giselle and Petja were inside out of the wet. He'd been watching Giselle earlier. She'd known it was going to rain and had been walking beside the wagon gathering firewood that she stowed in a sling that Josiah had rigged up under his wagon for just that purpose. It was comforting to know that when they finally did stop for the night, at least they'd not have too much trouble making a hot dinner. Mose was right. She was a good woman.

When they finally made it into camp, they were several miles short of what he had hoped to travel that day. Giselle and Petja had them a good hot dinner in next to no time, and once again Trace was grateful for their help. They had their chores done and were settling in for the night long before the other teamsters were even close. He put a canvas ground cover down before laying out their bedding under the wagon, and then put another one over top of them to protect them from the damp. It

55

took her a second to figure out how to pray without displacing everything, and he laughed with her as he held it still so that she could kneel.

Lying down that night with her was singularly comforting. It felt like they were in a cocoon, safe from the whole rest of the world, and they lay there all but snuggling next to each other and listened to the rain on the canvas wagon cover. Snug and warm, it was almost a soothing sound that lulled them to sleep like a lullaby. As he drifted off, he marveled at how good it was to work together as a couple to accomplish a common goal.

He'd never worked beside a woman like he was doing here, and the fact that working together proved to be so much more efficient than the other teamsters was somewhat puzzling to him. Shouldn't having the women along have been an extra burden and not a help? It had proved to be a great help to him and Mose, and as he prayed that night, he said an extra thank you for both Petja and Giselle. Especially Giselle.

That was the first night that they heard prairie wolves. The rain had been steady enough that they didn't hear them until almost morning, but once the rain tapered off, the mournful howling seemed like it was right in camp. They woke Trace up and then Dog growled and Giselle woke up as well. She looked over at him with wide eyes and he knew that she was thinking about Henry Filson. The wolves howling again took her mind off of Filson, but then he could tell she was afraid of the wolves instead.

Trace sleepily reached for her hand, and then when the howling came a third time, she rolled over against him and he wrapped an arm around her as before. That seemed to be all she needed to feel secure enough to go right back to sleep, but her proximity made sleep hard for him and it took him a while. When he finally got back to sleep with her there in his arms, the two intermittent nights finally clobbered him.

The next morning she was up and gone and Mose had to come and roust him to wake him up. "Come on sleeping beauty.

You waiting for breakfast in bed? What? Did you have to hug her again?"

Trace smiled tiredly. "It was my husbandly duty to protect her from the wolves."

"You probably hated that. Poor boy. You'd better get your lazy self outta bed. This train's leaving. With or without you. Lying there alone, you don't have much excuse for being left behind. You being the leader and all."

He sighed, "All right, all right. You're standing on my shirt, you big oaf. Move so I can get up. Why'd you let me sleep this long, anyway?"

Mose grinned, "When I came by the first time, you two were pretty snuggly. I figured you would hurt me if I woke you."

"Waking me I could handle. It's letting her go that would get you injured."

"Does she know that?"

"Heck, no! I'm far too afraid to tell her that. We gonna get more rain today?"

"You? Afraid? You laugh in the face of danger."

"Danger maybe; Giselle terrifies me. Where are my boots?"

"You didn't look too terrified earlier."

"No one's terrified when they're asleep, you numbskull. But you didn't see me when I was awake. I was positively petrified. And perfectly comfortable. There was no way I was movin'."

Mose looked at him. "You better get that grin off your face before she sees you. You look disgusting."

He pulled his boots on and swung his gun belt around his hips. "You jealous, Mose?"

Mose shook his head. "No. I still love Callie too much to be jealous. Just happy for you. But I'm sure I never had that sappy, mindless look when I was in love."

"Sappy? Mindless? Oh brother! Do I really look that bad?"

They stood up and Mose looked at him. "Yeah. Pretty much." He looked up as Giselle headed their way with Trace's breakfast. "You're gonna get busted, too."

She came up to them and stopped to look at Trace for a second. "You okay, Trace? You look a little... I don't know. Strange."

Mose laughed and Trace said, "What do you mean? Strange?"

"I don't know." She paused, studying him. "Strange happy. I brought you your breakfast since you didn't come in, so I can clean up." She handed him the plate and cup and then leaned under the wagon and began folding the canvases and rolling their beds. Mose began to chuckle and then coughed to disguise it as he walked away. Trace shook his head and smiled and walked around to set his cup on the wagon tongue. Between not sleeping and then being teased, these two were going to kill him.

CHAPTER 5

Trace was on horseback again that day and it was a good thing. They'd crossed any number of streams, and the Platte river a couple of times, but today it was high from the rain and it got a little rough before everyone was safely across. They would probably have lost Josiah's calf if Trace hadn't rescued it from horseback as it was swept away. Back safely on relatively dry ground on the far side of the river, he took a minute to stop and say a prayer of thanks that everyone was safe before heading back out on the trail.

Later that afternoon, they saw their first buffalo of the trip. The vast numbers of the past were mostly gone now, but there were still some huge herds that roamed the plains and this was one of them. It was probably the reason they'd heard the wolves last night. The wolf pack was likely hanging around the herd, waiting to pick off a calf or sickly old bull. While the animals were still just a black shadow on the western horizon, Trace rode over near Josiah's wagon. He wanted to see the VanKomens' faces when they saw their first buffalo herd. The massive beasts were probably something these kindly Dutch folks had never seen before.

As the afternoon wound down, the black shadow grew and sharpened until finally it became a herd of individual, shaggy, black and brown creatures. Giselle's eyes grew wide as the first wagons headed into the gap created when the buffalo gave way to the approaching wagon train. There were thousands of them on both sides for nearly as far as the eye could see, and as soon as the last wagon passed, the gap gradually closed back up and the train was entirely swallowed by the sea of ragged black.

Dark fell before they were out of the herd; Trace had them continue on until the buffalo petered out before circling to make camp. The buffalo probably wouldn't have even noticed if they had camped in their midst, but their own stock would have been skittish and a herd that size could have literally wiped their camps out if they had decided to stampede. For that matter, they still could, but at least out of the middle of the herd the wagon train was safer.

Trace had them circle on a hill above a small stream. As they were setting up camp, he heard something further up the water course and he went to investigate.

Half a mile away, off by themselves, was a buffalo trio consisting of a young bull, a cow, and a calf, hanging out in the willows on the creek bank. The young bull and cow were grunting and pawing the mud and dust up over their backs, while the four hundred and fifty pound calf of the year grazed nearby.

Sneaking to within sixty yards of them, Trace shot the calf and then headed back to camp to get a team of mules to bring it in. After he and Mose cleaned, skinned and quartered it, they brought the meat and hide back into camp to cut up and distribute.. Fresh meat was always appreciated out on the trail. He spread the hide out, hair side down, to dry. Later he would try to trade it to an Indian at one of the trading posts or forts.

Giselle was fascinated by the buffalo, and even the slaughtering process—although Trace wondered for a second if she was going to be sick again. She was looking a little green around the gills when she headed off to bed. Early the next morning, she asked him to take her and show her the great beast's innards. He thought that was strange, but he agreed and helped her up on the back of his horse and took her to see it.

She walked around the huge, smelly gut pile, and taking a stick, tried to poke around to inspect every little thing about it. Finally, Trace began to point out the different parts of it, explaining what each was and what it did in the animal's body. She was inordinately interested in it and, finally, he asked her why.

She smiled a little self consciously. "I've always wanted to see something like this. Home in Holland the only time that I saw meat was when it was served. I wanted to see what everything looked like and did, but my father believed that terribly unladylike and was actually somewhat embarrassed that his daughter was curious about that type of thing. He wanted me to be well-dressed and well-mannered and not well-educated.

"Even here in America, I've only seen meat after it's all cut up. You should be grateful that your father encouraged your formal education. How marvelous to know, not only about animals, but about the human body as well. Our Father in Heaven has given us wonderful bodies that are miraculous in the way they function." She hesitated. "At least I think so."

Helping her back onto the horse, he said, "I think so too. I'm not only fascinated, but I have this need to fix it as well. There's something in me that makes me a doctor. I've been that way since I was a child. Unlike you, my father encouraged me to dissect and study everything. Animal, plant, chemical. It didn't matter. He wanted me to understand it all and I thought that was just dandy.

"I dragged Mose along with me for most everything. At first he thought I was torturing him to make him learn it all, especially after the fact that my mother made him wear shoes. When he came to live with us when he was seven, he'd never worn a pair of shoes in his life. In Georgia it was warm, and he didn't think he should have to wear shoes unless his feet were cold. I'm afraid they butted heads over the shoe thing."

She laughed her musical laugh almost in his ear. "Knowing Mose, your mother must have been a strong woman to win that battle."

"My mother is definitely strong, but that's a good thing. She had to be strong to stand up to the bigotry there and adopt a young slave boy into her family. That wasn't done in Georgia seventeen years ago. That's still not done in Georgia."

Sadly, Giselle said, "That is a shame. How long will it be before we all learn to love and value each other? When

61

that lamb will lie down with the lion and Christ can come back again?"

He shook his head. "Sometimes I wonder if we humans will ever figure it out, Elle."

She hugged him around the waist. "Some have always had it figured out, Trace. And you're right. Some never will. But we must do the best we can to help each other learn. As Mose would say, 'It's what Jesus would want.'"

Back in camp, they had to hurry in order to not make the other wagons wait for them. Petja had made breakfast and Josiah had milked the cow, and they headed out as soon as they could. In her hurry, Giselle didn't eat enough, and by lunch, between the hunger and the interesting guts she had looked at that morning, she was horribly ill. Petja knew that she felt awful and encouraged her to stay in the back of the wagon, where she brought food to her.

That night, she struggled to make it through chores and went straight down to bed. Even at that, she had to get up to be sick in the night. When she came back to bed, Trace asked her sleepily if she was okay, and she told him she was fine, but she didn't feel that way. She felt awful. She tried to ignore the nausea and even resorted to dwelling on Trace lying next to her to keep her mind off of the way she felt.

They had been on the trail for just over a month and a half. They had made it through the dust, the rivers, and the buffalo. They'd struggled to find feed, avoid quicksand and had repaired innumerable wagon issues. They'd even learned to deal with the stubborn mule and the quarrelsome freighters. She and Trace had become fast friends, and both he and Mose felt like her family now. But she still hadn't told him about the babies.

She was almost sure there were two of them. She never dreamed about just one. She was almost four months along now, and her dresses had all been let out to accommodate her growing tummy. It almost didn't seem like just her tummy. Even her ribs and chest were expanding.

She was starting to feel guilty about not telling him, as close as they had become, but every time she thought about doing it, she couldn't bring herself to. She wasn't sure why. She just didn't think that she could explain, and she didn't want to see the pity or revulsion that she feared in his eyes.

They had been traveling primarily over the flats of the Great Plains, and it had indeed been a great plain. From time to time, there were streams and small hills and washes, but for the most part it, had been a long, flat, monotonous pull. She had long ago learned to pick up buffalo droppings and toss them into the sling under the wagon to use for fuel for the cooking fires. That was the only option they had because trees were so rare here. She had learned to handle whatever had come her way, except for her feelings for Trace.

She feared that she had fallen in love with him, which was senseless beyond belief, but try as she might, she didn't seem to be able to tell her heart to keep its distance. She was close to her grandparents, but she couldn't even tell them what she was feeling and was trying to figure out how to fix this all by herself. Wondering how to do that, when she'd never felt this strongly in her life, made her feel even younger than her seventeen years. Younger and more foolish than she had ever thought herself.

At least they were making good progress. They were nearing the halfway point from what she understood. Although the lateness of their trip was making feed hard to find, it was a relatively dry time of year and travel had been dusty, but steady.

They'd come more than half of the distance, but the flat prairie they'd been traveling would go faster than the hills and mountains and canyons when they reached them. The next day they were to reach something called Chimney Rock, and not far after that would be Fort Laramie and the first real settlement they had encountered in weeks.

In a way, she wanted this trip to last forever because she didn't want Trace to be gone from her life, but in another way, the sooner they reached their destination, the less watching him drive away from her would hurt. Already it was going to kill her. By that same token, she wasn't sure if she should be doing everything that she could to distance herself from him, or enjoying every minute that she had with him like it was a precious treasure that would soon run out. She'd prayed for wisdom, but her heart and her head seemed to be scrambling all of her personal inspiration.

Unsure of what to do, she turned on her side restlessly and then scooted close enough to him to just touch him with her elbow. Even that little contact with him was comforting and she was finally able to get back to sleep.

The next morning, Trace was up and gone as usual when Mose showed up with a concerned face to deliver his lifesaving biscuit. She thanked him gratefully. "What would I ever do without you, Mose?"

He stayed bent down to talk to her before he turned back around to leave. "You'd be fine. Just fine, Miss Giselle. Maybe you'd even drum up the guts to tell your husband why you're sick. You need to. He's going to be both mad and hurt when he finds out. The longer you go, the worse he's going to feel."

She nodded guiltily. "You're right, Mose. I know you are. I just can't figure out how to go about it. It won't matter soon anyway. It won't be long before it's glaringly obvious. I can hardly bend to climb under here without ripping out my dresses already." He didn't say anything, just looked at her steadily and she wanted to squirm. "I'll figure it out, Mose. As soon as I can. Honest."

He nodded and looked up. "Now would be a good time. Here he comes." With that, he stood up and walked away, pausing to talk to Trace for a second as they passed.

A second later, she saw Trace's head appear under the edge of the wagon box. He noticed her biscuit and said, "Hey, what is this? Breakfast in bed? Hop out of there and I'll roll up our gear and stow it."

She knew she couldn't get right up just then. She'd have thrown up on Trace's lap. She groaned inwardly. "Can I have just another minute or two, Trace? I'll be up in a second, I promise."

He looked at her quizzically. "Sure. Whatever. Is something wrong?"

She glanced up to where Mose had just disappeared and sighed. "No. I'm fine. Sometimes I'm just a bit slow moving when I wake up. Give me a small moment and I'll be up."

He followed her glance after Mose and wondered what he was missing. "Take as long as you want, Elley. I'll do some other stuff before the bedding."

She nodded and he stood back up. He paused for a second. Something wasn't right with her, but she didn't appear to want to talk to him about it. On a hunch he went to hunt up Mose. On finding him building a fire, he asked him point blank, "Was there something wrong with Giselle this morning?"

Mose looked back at him steadily and asked, "What did she say to you?"

"Nothing, why? She just said she wanted me to give her another couple minutes in bed. But it was kind of weird. She seemed almost sad when I asked if she was okay. What's wrong?"

Shaking his head, Mose said, "Nothing's *wrong*. Maybe she's just still tired. Did she sleep okay?"

Trace thought about that while he looked from his best friend to his own wagon and back. "I don't know. She got up once, but I was tired enough that as soon as I knew she was back, I went back to sleep." Mose was almost acting guilty or something, and Trace suddenly had a thought that really bothered him. He looked Mose right in the face and asked, "What's going on, Mose? Why are both of you acting strange? There's not something between you and Giselle is there?"

Mose looked him squarely in the eyes and said earnestly, "Of course not, Trace. Not only is she your wife, but I would never do something like that. If you think about it, you know that."

"I didn't think you would. So what is going on? Is something going on?"

After hesitating a few seconds, Mose looked out at the lightening horizon. "If something is going on, Trace, it's going on with her. There's nothing that has anything to do with me."

Still confused, Trace said, "Okay... So do I ask her? Or what?"

Mose looked back at him and smiled. "I'm not the official expert on what to do if women act strange, Trace. Maybe she's just a little under the weather. Ask her. Or wait until she volunteers something. I don't know. Who does know about women?"

Trace sighed. "Not me. That's for sure."

He was still standing there thinking a few minutes later when Giselle walked up with a perfectly normal and pleasant, "Good morning," and started getting ready to cook breakfast. Trace glanced over at Mose who raised his eyebrows and shrugged. More confused than ever, Trace went and rolled the bedding and went back to morning chores to get ready to go. Jehosaphat! How had the men of this species muddled through this woman thing since the beginning of time? He was completely lost! Something had been wrong. He was sure of it. But apparently she was fine now.

Giselle felt guilty the whole morning and probably would have all afternoon as well except that a couple of striking things happened. Just after lunch as they were traveling, her grandmother turned to her grandfather and said, "Josiah. I do believe it's time that you baptized me into the Church."

Giselle was floored, but her grandfather didn't seem the least bit surprised. "Very well, Petja. We aren't where we can ask the brethren for their approval, but I'm sure they would give us their blessing. We shall take care of you as soon as we come to another stream, dear."

Giselle didn't say anything, just sat there in shock. She had finally come to the conclusion that her grandmother would never be baptized in this life and she would have to do that work for her after she was dead.

After all they had been through with the Saints and the Mormons haters and the mobs and the cold and disease, she'd been convinced that if her grandmother was going to join them, she would have already done it long ago. It had actually been good that she hadn't, because her non-Mormon status and the fact that Josiah had been willing to support and love her anyway-and accompany her to different churches-had been the reason he had been successful in obtaining some of the Saints' money for their lands.

As Giselle thought about that, she wondered if that hadn't been the Lord's plan all along. As soon as she had that thought, she was sure of it. Somehow, her grandparents had been in tune with the Spirit enough to let God use them for his purposes with a happy heart, and now it was all working out in the end. Giselle sat there on the wagon seat beside them and started to cry. She tried to stop, but she couldn't do a thing about the tears that streamed down her face.

Her grandfather noticed her sobbing and reached to put a patient and kind arm around her with a knowing smile. "It's been a long time coming, hasn't it Giselle, dear. But I never doubted that it would. The Lord needed your grandmother to help His saints in their time of need. Her work is now done and He wants her safely in his fold before she does anything more in this life."

Even the fact that they saw their first ever real Indian didn't stop the emotional storm that fell from her eyes. She watched as the group of three mounted Indians came down and met with Trace and Mose and John a little ways out from the wagon train, but still her tears flowed down her cheeks. She had heard that expecting a baby made women cry, but after more than an hour she felt foolish. Yet she couldn't do anything but blow her nose and wipe her eyes.

The Indians came and talked and then left peaceably, and when they went into their camp circle that night, Trace didn't seem nearly as concerned about them as he was about Giselle crying on and off all the way through making and eating dinner. Before she was even finished eating, he sent her to go lie down on the bedding he had already put out for her, promising her that he'd take care of the cow for her that night.

When he came to bed an hour later, she was still a little weepy and he put a hand to her cheek and asked, "Are you going to be okay, Elley? Is this the same thing that made you upset this morning or is this something else?"

He could tell that she was deciding what to tell him and wondered if she would level with him this time. Finally, she said as she dissolved into tears again, "My grandmother is finally going to join the Church, Trace. After being willing to leave all of her family, dealing with the mobs and this mess with me, and struggling to make it to Zion. After everything, she's still going to become a member. Finally. I know you don't understand that or what a big deal it is to us, but it... it... it matters so much to me."

Gently he asked, "Then what are you so upset about?"

"Oh, Trace. I'm not upset. I'm happy. I just can't seem to get these emotions under control very well."

He thought to himself, *you can say that again*. To her he said, "Is there anything I can do to help you?"

"No." She shook her head and sniffled. "Just don't be upset with me for crying so much. I can't help it. I'll be fine in the morning. Just be patient."

"Patience I can do. It's trying to figure you out that has me hoodooed."

Feeling guilty again for not leveling with him about her babies, she said, "Sorry. Sometimes I can't even figure myself out, so I know what you mean."

He laughed and put an arm around her to pull her close to him. "We'll figure you out eventually. Between the two of us, we should be able to at least do that. G'night, Giselle."

"Good night, Trace."

CHAPTER 6

The next morning, Trace was kind of keeping an eye out for her. He wondered how she was going to be today after being such an emotional mess last night. She was still in her bed when he saw Mose approach their wagon and duck down and hand her something and then walk away. Trace couldn't see what it was, and Mose hadn't said anything to her unless it was a word or two. At any rate, a few minutes later she appeared at the fire looking beautiful as ever and ready to start the day. He was glad. He'd been worried that she'd cry again.

That afternoon, they reached Chimney Rock and stopped for a while to explore a little and add their names to those already written there by earlier settlers. Giselle signed hers "Giselle V. Grayson" and for some reason, Trace loved that. He signed his right below it with pride, wishing that their marriage days weren't numbered like they were.

That night there were coyotes yipping and howling all around them and Dog started to growl again and woke her up. She rolled over close to Trace and tensed to listen and then asked, "What is it?"

He put a hand comfortingly on her back, "They're coyotes. Wild dogs that are smaller and much less dangerous than the wolves."

"What a strange sound. Why do they do that?"

"It's probably either that they're hunting or they're just singing to the moon. I don't know. I love to hear them, though."

Dog growled again and Giselle laughed softly. "Dog doesn't." She yawned, sighed against him, and closed her eyes again. "Maybe they got mixed up and sang us awake instead of to sleep."

Trace smiled into the dark. "Maybe."

They camped the next night beside a beautiful, clear stream. Josiah left as soon as the wagons had stopped and walked up the stream bank and out of sight. That night, after dinner was cleaned up, he gave the women their shawls and took Petja and Giselle out of camp for a walk.

Once out of hearing of the others, he told them that he'd found a place where he could baptize Petja. They continued on, and at length they got to the place where Giselle finally got to see her grandfather baptize his dear wife. They were only in their white underclothing, but it was a sweet and sacred experience that had Giselle in tears once again. She struggled to have her emotions well in hand again before they made it back to camp, and Trace only looked at her for a few minutes without saying anything when she came to bed.

Within a few days of leaving Chimney Rock, they pulled the wagon train to a camp site outside of Fort Laramie. They were planning to camp there for a day or two before moving on. Once things were set up, most of the teamsters headed into the settlement and Josiah and the two women went in as well. There were a few things that they were hoping they could buy there, but mostly they just wanted to see real people and buildings. It felt like it had been years since Giselle had seen civilization.

At the trading post she bought fabric to make a couple of new dresses that would accommodate her tummy that was getting distinctly thicker although, so far, she had tried to hide it. Maybe as they rode she could sew. And she bought candy. She had always had a sweet tooth, and she had missed candy this last couple of months. On a whim, she bought some for Trace and Mose and some that her grandparents loved as well.

Watching her sweet grandparents visit with some other settlers in the store, she was so glad for them. She knew that they were both friendly by nature and loved this sort of thing.

Two days later when both of them came down sick, she wasn't so glad for them, and wished that they had skipped all the visiting and not come in contact with others. At first they were just achy and tired, and then a day or two later, they came down with fevers that started out relatively mild. Giselle assumed they just had summer colds, and she was glad that they'd used enough of the supplies they'd brought to have room for them to sleep in the back of the wagon as she drove the team.

Trace noticed that she was driving alone as he rode along on his horse and came by to check on them. Even he didn't think too much about them being ill. Their symptoms were relatively mild, and the two of them were still cheerful and positive even though they were a little under the weather.

Morning and evening chores were more demanding when she did them alone, and she had to go to bed later and get up earlier in order to get everything done, but she did it and felt confident that she could handle this for a couple of days while they recuperated. On the second day that she drove alone, it started to rain. Her grandfather had an oilskin slicker but she couldn't stop driving to dig it out until lunch time, and she pulled a shawl up around her shoulders instead.

By lunch time, she was soaked through and spent the time they were stopped changing into dry clothes and attending to her grandparents. Then she tried to eat her own lunch as she drove, but it didn't work out so well. The food was soggy from the rain within minutes and the road had become slippery with mud; and she soon set her plate aside to focus on her team. The one stubborn mule had gotten much easier to deal with during the trip, but on days like today, it was sullen and intractable.

There had been no one to gather firewood and stow it in the sling under the wagon to keep dry to start the fire that night. Dinner was a little later than usual. By the time she had it cleaned up, Trace had already milked her cow and had spread their bedding out. She was still cold from her morning soaking and longed to snuggle next to him to get warm but didn't dare. For some reason, the sound of the rain on the canvas wasn't comforting this time.

Tonight, for the first time, she wondered if what ailed Josiah and Petja was indeed just a cold. This was the fourth day they'd been sick, and their aches and fevers had escalated to such terribly sore throats that they could hardly swallow. A nagging fever chilled them and tired them to listlessness. Neither one of them had been interested in food and had hardly even taken notice when she spoke to them.

They were into the month of September, and even though they had made good time so far, they had some mountains to go through yet, and she knew they could already have snow this early. Just the thought made her already-chilled skin break out in goose bumps.

She was still sleeping like the dead in the morning when Mose came by, and she was loathe to leave the warm cocoon of her blankets when she dragged her tired body up. It was still drizzling rain and she put Josiah's slicker on from the get go, but then struggled to do her work even with the too long sleeves rolled up. They finally got started. At least she had been ready before some of the other teamsters that were dealing with the same wet wood and damp that slowed her.

As she drove, she prayed. Her grandparents were gravely ill and this morning there had been no denying that fact. They were lying in the back of the wagon in a lethargic stupor and she feared for what Trace would say when he looked at them. At lunch he came to the wagon to get lunch and she asked him to see what he thought. He'd been smiling when he approached, but the smile was replaced with a look that was frighteningly grim when he climbed back out of the wagon after examining them.

"Giselle, I'm sorry that I haven't kept closer watch over them. How long have they been like this?"

"Last night they weren't much interested in eating or visiting, but they've only been this bad this morning."

He came to her and was far too earnest for comfort when he tried to explain. "Elle, they're sick. Very sick. They have something called Throat Distemper and they have a serious case of it. We'll have to make sure that they get enough food and liquid down, and more importantly, that they can breathe okay. It makes a leathery membrane cover their throats and makes breathing difficult at best."

She looked up at him in the rain and asked him right out, "Will they die?"

He didn't flinch as he told her honestly, "It's possible as bad as they are, but not likely. But, Elley, this is highly contagious. When you're helping them you need to wear a handkerchief over your nose and mouth because you could contract it as well. And wash your hands. Always wash your hands. It's not known how it spreads exactly, but it can become epidemic if not handled correctly. I'll help you care for them, but be careful, okay? I don't want you sick as well."

She nodded and looked down, surprised by the tender note in his voice. It took her a minute to focus and to go wash her hands before getting their lunch out of the basket. Half of her wanted to sit down and bawl over what he had just told her, but knowing that he was truly concerned for her helped ease that a little.

That afternoon as she drove, she continued to pray. And not just for her grandparents. She prayed for herself as well, that when the time came for her to say goodbye to Trace and Mose, that she wouldn't just melt into a puddle of heartbreak.

Over the past months, she had come at first to lean on him and now there was no doubt that she was far too attached to him. She hesitated to use the words *in love*, even in her head, but if she was honest with herself, that's what was happening to her heart. She knew it was completely foolish under the circumstances and in a way, she felt guilty as well for being in love with someone that wasn't a member of the Church. At least the fact that they would be going their separate ways in a matter of a few weeks dealt with that.

The wind picked up toward evening, and by the time they circled into camp, it was a veritable gale blowing the rain straight sideways. Trying to get the dinner fire lit in the wind and using wet wood took the teamwork of all three of them, and even then it seemed to take forever.

By the time they had hot food, she was nearly too tired to eat it and merely picked at hers before giving the remainder to Dog. She hurried to milk the cow and then finally lay down to rest beside Trace, literally exhausted. Her prayers that night were sincere but short. She was grateful, but she needed divine intervention.

Wolves howling again in the middle of the night woke her out of her deep sleep, but this time, she was so weary that she had to let the fear go. She moved against Trace, grateful beyond belief for his strength and reassurance and went right back to her slumber.

As she milked the cow the next morning, she began having the strangest ache in her lower back. Once she was settled on the wagon seat to drive the ache went away again, but then late that afternoon it returned. This time it was her back and stomach and she worried that she was getting the same aches and fatigue that her grandparents had. She did her best to ignore it as she worked at the evening chores.

Lying down eased the strain in her back and she felt much better after just a few minutes of resting beside Trace. She wished that she could ask how he thought Josiah and Petja were doing, but she was actually afraid to ask. They didn't seem to be a lot worse, but she knew that they were no better either. She would have dearly loved to have a priesthood blessing for them, but unfortunately, the only one here that held the priesthood was one of the ones that needed its power so desperately.

It had only been raining off and on for five days, but it felt like a hundred by the time she made it to bed the next night. The pain in her lower back and stomach had nagged at her all day and tonight when she had changed for bed, she found that she had been spotting blood. For the first time she recognized that the ache she had been feeling was female cramps and not the illness that her grandparents were suffering with, and the huge relief that she felt to know that she wasn't coming down with Throat Distemper almost made her feel guilty. At least Josiah and Petja seemed to be somewhat improved this evening.

The pain went away after lying down again, and she rested better than she had in days; and even more rain the next morning didn't discourage her like it had the last day or two. Using wood that she'd put under her grandparents' wagon to dry, she got breakfast started and hurried to milk the cow and clean up afterward.

Climbing up into the wagon, she fed her grandparents and helped them both to sit up to drink as much as they possibly could. They were sweetly gracious about her caring for them, and she hoped what she was seeing was indeed improvement and not just wishful thinking.

She was determined this morning to stow wood before they left this camp so that this evening wouldn't be such a struggle as the last couple. This morning the ache in her back started before they even set out as she rushed to and from the nearby stand of trees carrying the loads of wood. As the wagon train headed out onto the trail, she could feel herself spotting again, and this time she wondered if everything was okay with her babies. She'd spotted a little from time to time through the whole four and a half months that she'd been in this condition, but she didn't remember ever spotting this much.

Trying to push the worry from her mind because there was nothing that she could do about any of it, she tried to concentrate on what she could do. She mentally went over her responsibilities as she drove, trying to plan and streamline things as much as possible. Perhaps with better planning, she could make things run more smoothly than they had been since her grandparents had taken ill. She certainly hoped so. She had begun to feel like she was falling behind in pulling her weight and her grandparents' as well.

She bled enough that morning that, at lunch, she had to climb into the wagon and change clothes before heading back onto the trail that afternoon. Her grandmother woke up as she was changing, and Giselle asked her about the bleeding and if this much was normal. Even as sick as she was, Petja seemed concerned and told her that she didn't think it was okay. She was upset enough about it that Giselle decided asking had been a mistake and resolved to protect them from worry better in the future.

It had been a good theory, but over the next several days, the hemorrhaging continued and got worse to the point that there was no hiding it from either of her grandparents. In fact, even with padding her underclothing with toweling rags, it took changing her petticoats and slips multiple times a day to keep Trace and Mose and the others from knowing as well.

At length, Petja told her with a deep sadness in her voice, "I'm afraid that you may be losing your baby, my dear. I don't know what else would be causing this severe of bleeding. And here we lay unable to even help in your time of need. I'm so sorry, dear Elle. Please forgive your grandfather and me for our weakness."

Giselle leaned to kiss her soft forehead. "You must worry about getting better and not about me, Nanna. The good Lord will watch over me. He is aware of all of this and I have faith that He will help me." She patted the small bulge under her dress. "We will be fine. You'll see. Just get yourself better, do you hear me?" She tried to pretend to be scolding, but could never have sounded stern with these two dear people that had been willing to give up everything to accompany her here to America.

She had been having to spend the noon time in helping her grandparents eat and then changing her underclothing. Her mid-day meal had become only a bite or two, if she had time for even that as the train got under way again. She assumed it was skipping this meal that was making her feel so weak and light-headed when she went to stand up, and she told herself that she would do better about eating. One good thing was that she had become more slender, and the dresses that had been threatening to rip had become looser again. This was indeed a blessing because she hadn't been able to start making any bigger dresses since she'd bought the fabric at Fort Laramie those weeks ago.

Twice that week in the evenings, she heated water in the big kettle and did laundry to wash out her petticoats, but she still found herself resorting to borrowing some of Petja's to tide her over between launderings.

What had started out as intermittent spotting had progressed to steady bleeding. It had been happening for nine days when Trace stopped her one morning as she made breakfast and stood looking at her for a second before asking. "Are you okay, Elley? You don't have your usual color in your cheeks."

She simply smiled and said, "It must be all that rain last week. I had gotten shamefully brown on this trip. Being paler is much more proper for women anyway." Trace looked a little skeptical, but didn't comment further.

It felt good to be asked after. The pace of the train had picked up with the cooling of the weather into fall, the rougher terrain and the shorter days. The men had been as busy trying to push on as quickly as possible as she had been caring for Josiah and Petja. She and Trace rarely had time to visit anymore, except for a few quiet words spoken before they dropped off to sleep from exhaustion at night.

As hard as the rigorous pace had become, it did help her to put her feelings for Trace into better perspective. There hadn't been time to think about how much she enjoyed him, or how much she would have liked to be a real wife, when every waking moment had been used up.

Even sleeping had become an urgent need that left little energy for dreams or wakefulness, regardless of what fearful things lurked in the dark. The wolves and coyotes no longer frightened her because she always knew that Trace was there beside her. His strength had taken most of her fears of physical dangers away completely.

Now if she could just find a way to make getting up in the mornings a little easier. Waking and getting up had become a grueling feat. The fatigue from working too hard and not eating or sleeping enough had become almost overwhelming. Sometimes she wondered if she would have ever made it up if it hadn't been for Mose coming by with her cold biscuit.

One morning he commented on it. He'd bent to wake her, and when she finally groaned and opened her eyes, he studied her for a minute and then said, "Miss Giselle, you need to tell Trace. He's going to be one offended husband when he does find out. And he'd make you take it easier than you've been if he knew, which would be a good thing."

She struggled to sit up and leaned against the wagon wheel for a minute until she wasn't so light-headed and replied, "You're wrong, Mose. I need to do more, not less. You've heard the stories of the Donner and Reed party in forty-six in the California mountains. Granted, they used less judgment than you and Trace, but still, delay could cost your lives. Or all of ours if we don't make it over the Rocky Mountains in time. I can't be whining and asking to be babied. Especially with my grandparents already not helping."

For once Mose put his foot down. In a voice that brooked no argument he said, "No, Miss Giselle. It's past time. I'll give you another two days. If you haven't told him, which is your place and you know it, then I will. And in the meantime, I'm going to be taking over milking that cow and caring for your chickens. Enough is enough."

Honestly, she didn't have the energy to argue. "Okay, Mose. I'll tell him. And thank you for your help. I'll accept it gladly." He left and she sighed. How was she ever going to tell Trace?

Even though he couldn't hear what was being said, Trace was surprised to hear the tone of voice that Mose was using with Giselle. Mose was incredibly even-tempered. In all his life, Trace had never heard him talk to a woman in any kind of a short tone. This morning he sounded like her father reprimanding her. When Mose came back over to their wagon, Trace asked him about it. "What's going on? What are you upset with Giselle about?"

Mose glanced over to where she was starting breakfast and said, "I'm sorry, Trace. I'm not at liberty to say what I'm upset about. You might ask Miss Giselle though. She could tell you."

Surprised that he wouldn't say more than that, Trace went to help Giselle at the fire and asked her the same thing. She paused for a moment like she was thinking, and then shook her head and turned away. "He's just upset because he thinks there are some things that I should be doing that I'm not. I'll take care of it." She leaned down to turn the hot cakes on her griddle.

Trace wasn't sure whether to delve or not. Somehow, he'd almost gotten the impression from Mose that he needed to know whatever it was that they had been talking so heatedly about, but Giselle didn't seem to think that way. Wondering what to do and what his role was here, he let it go for the time being. Later he'd pick at Mose a little more for answers.

In the meantime, Giselle looked awful and he worried about her. He crouched down beside her and took her pancake turner. When she looked up at him, he said, "At least your grandparents don't seem to be getting any worse. How are you doing? Are you holding out taking care of them? I know that caring for the sick can be hard at times."

Stirring a pan of scrambled eggs, she didn't look up at him as she said, "I'm fine, but thank you for asking. How are we doing traveling? Are we going to make it over the mountains on time?"

That was a good question, but only God truly knew the answer. "We're traveling as fast as we can. Whether that will prove to be fast enough will depend completely on what kind of fall we have. If the weather stays good, we'll be fine. If winter hits early, we'll be in trouble either this side of the valley of the Great Salt Lake or in the mountains on the other side. Either way, we need to go as fast as we can."

Finally, she looked up. "I've been praying that all will be well. I'll keep praying."

"I will too, Elle. I will too."

He was surprised to see Mose milking her cow, and later as Trace rode his horse beside the train, he came alongside Mose's wagon. For several minutes he just rode with him in silence. Finally, Mose asked, "Did she say anything when you asked?"

Trace was noncommittal. "About as much as you did when I asked. Why were you milking this morning?"

"Because I think she's doing too much and I'm worried about her. When I try to encourage her to go easier she always brings up the danger of getting caught in the snow in the mountains."

Thoughtfully, Trace said, "Yeah, she said something about that to me, too. She's looking a little rough lately. I mean as rough as a woman that beautiful can look. Is that what's wrong? She's doing too much?"

Mose shrugged. "You're the doctor. You tell me. A little rough isn't what I'm seeing. I'm seeing full blown exhausted."

Trace was quiet for a while, thinking. He hadn't noticed her all that exhausted, but then maybe he just wasn't seeing things very clearly. She always looked great to him. Too great. His feelings for her had become so strong that he'd begun to almost try to avoid her to dampen them. How he was ever going to be able to walk away from her to continue on to California was beyond him, the way he felt about her.

He thought back to what Mose had said about her. Trace knew that she was sleeping hard lately, and for a while he'd wondered if she was putting on weight, but lately her face was almost too slender. And she was paler, but she had attributed that to the rain and Trace had accepted that logic. He decided that come lunch time, he would look at her more closely, and see what he really thought.

As Giselle drove that morning, she felt horrible. Her whole body ached from the cramps in her stomach and lower back, and she felt ridiculously guilty for telling Trace that she was fine. That was the closest to telling an outright lie that she had ever come.

Even telling herself that it was necessary to keep things running as smoothly with the wagon train as possible didn't make it seem any less dishonest. She wasn't fine, and the blood that she knew was soaking through her petticoats and skirt right now was more than evidence of that.

She wondered how much a person could bleed before it would make them sick. In a way, she knew that Mose was right and that she needed to tell Trace right away, but if what her grandmother suspected was true and she'd lost these babies, then telling him would be pointless anyway.

She was dizzy and light-headed and almost nauseous today, and with the pain, she could be honest at least with herself and admit that she had never felt so weak and sick in her life. It was all she could do to hold onto the reins this morning, and every bump that the wagon hit made the pain in her back radiate outward. Several times she caught herself groaning when her tummy would cramp up, and she wished that she could rest during the coming noon instead of feeding and helping her grandparents.

Towards late morning, she began to know that something was seriously wrong, and when she found herself with black dots dancing in front of her eyes, she worried in earnest. She was too weak to call out to Mose in the wagon in front, and Trace was riding along somewhere behind. Neither of her grandparents were in any shape to help her, and when she knew that she was indeed blacking out, the only thing she could do was slip from the seat of the wagon to the floor in front of it, hoping that she wouldn't fall underneath the mules or the wheels.

CHAPTER 7

Trace had spent the morning scouting ahead for the best route for the day, and then riding up and down the length of the train checking with the drivers and the wagon master as he went. Everything seemed to be going well down the whole length of it, but still he couldn't shake this feeling that he was missing something that was out of place. Looking around for a clue to what was nagging him, he noticed that Giselle's wagon was pulling wide for some reason. He started forward to see what the problem was, but it pulled right back into place again and he held back.

Must be that stupid, ornery mule again. From time to time it got some fool notion in its head to act up, even after nearly two and a half months on the trail. He should have encouraged Josiah to sell it back in the settlements and get another that wouldn't be so much trouble. Twenty minutes later, she did it again, and this time the wagon pulled wide and then went back into line only to go wide the other direction. What was she doing? She'd been driving by herself for weeks now and she'd done a great job. He wondered why she was having trouble today.

He kicked his horse into a trot to go check with her. If he had his druthers, he'd ride right beside her all day, but that hadn't been much of an option and it wouldn't have been wise anyway. He had known all along that they would be parting ways in the Mormon's Zion, and falling so hard for her so fast had made him feel almost like he shouldn't spend time with her at all.

Coming up alongside her wagon, he was shocked to realize that she wasn't in the driver's seat, and he wondered what had happened that was such an emergency that she'd let the mules have their heads while she climbed into the back. He was just about to call out to her when he realized that she wasn't in the back at all, she was lying in a heap on the floor in front of the seat. One of the reins to the mule team was dangling over the front of the wagon and the other was dragging on the ground back under the wagon box itself. That was what was making the team veer left or right. Every time the dragging rein hung up on something, the team would pull that direction.

Instantly sick at heart and wondering what in the world had happened, he rode as close as he dared to the side of the wagon and then jumped from the horse and pulled himself up to the seat. The one rein was easy, but to get hold of the other he had to climb clear in front of the wagon and try to balance on the single trees in front of it. Even then he couldn't reach the rein and had to climb even further out over the wagon tongue. He was watching the rogue mule, wondering if he was going to be able to do this without the mule coming unglued at the seams.

Just when the mule pinned its ears and he thought to himself here he goes, he was able to catch the other rein. Now he just had to make it back onto the wagon without becoming tangled in the riggings and harness. When he finally made it back to the wagon seat, it felt like he'd been hanging precariously between the wagon and mules for days.

Abruptly, he pulled the wagon out of line and stopped the team. Putting the brake on and tying off the reins, he knelt to see what had happened to Giselle. When he went to pick her up, he was horrified to see that her dress was covered in blood. He stretched her out as best he could, but he was unable to tell where it was coming from. As the wagon behind him went past, he told his driver to hurry forward and tell Mose that he was pulling off to see to the VanKomens, and to go ahead to the nooning area and he'd catch up. "Oh, and see if you can catch my horse, would you."

He went to turn back to Giselle and Josiah leaned a weary head up over the wagon box to see what was going on.

Trace turned to him and asked without preamble, "Josiah, what's happened to Giselle? Where is she injured?" At first Josiah didn't appear to understand what he was asking. Frustrated, Trace asked again. "The blood, Josiah. Where is she cut?"

Tiredly, Josiah replied as he looked sadly at Giselle lying on the floor of the seat. "She's not cut, Trace. She's losing the baby."

Trace didn't understand what he was saying. "She's what?"

"The baby. For days she's been worried that she was going to lose it. The last couple of days especially." He sighed. "Petja and I have been heartbroken that we couldn't help her more."

Trace still couldn't comprehend what he was telling him. "Baby? What baby?" He narrowed his eyes as he looked at the old man, questioning. "Giselle is expecting a baby?"

Gently, Josiah began to explain in a voice filled with the deepest sadness. "Filson and a mob of Mormon haters came. Giselle either happened to be in the way, or she was what they were after in the first place. I do not know which. I only know that the baby was the result of them hurting her so badly that night."

Was he hearing what he was hearing? He couldn't seem to get his brain to process this. Giselle pregnant? And by a mob of hateful men that included Filson? He sat back on his heals stunned. How had he worked and slept beside her for months without figuring this out? He was a doctor for crying out loud! Slowly, Josiah lay back down in the wagon box while Trace looked down at the unconscious and bloody girl in his arms, stunned beyond even acting. His Giselle. How had he not known this?

Mose had known. Somehow Mose had known, but hadn't felt like he could tell him. And Giselle hadn't told him even though they were married and he was a doctor that should have been helping her. At first the feeling of failing miserably was overwhelming, but the very volume of the blood that she was lying in spurred him to action. He had seen her this morning. All of this had been from just the last few hours. This had been going on for days?

In retrospect, he remembered thinking that she had been changing dresses more often. Now he knew why.

But this wasn't something that he could fix with a few stitches. There were places in this country that they could operate on this kind of thing, but the wilds of the Wyoming territory wasn't one of them. The only thing he could do would be to put her down flat on her back and hope that the hemorrhaging would stop before she bled to death. He rose up to look over into the wagon box. All of the bedding in sight was being used by Josiah and Petja. Giselle's bedding was with his in his wagon ahead.

He looked around them at the country they were traveling through. It was a variable country between the baldness of the prairie and the mountains ahead. Hills and flats were interspersed with washes and gullies where streams ran through. Occasionally there had been bluffs and mesas, but immediately around them, it was just occasional low hills.

He tried to remember what the country was like directly ahead. He needed to pull off somewhere and take care of these three, but where? Where could he safely let them rest up where she wouldn't have to be moved and jostled around? He had to find some shelter. He couldn't bed her down in the back near her grandparents even if he'd been able to somehow find the room because they were so contagious. He'd have to keep going at least long enough to find a place to get her in out of the weather.

While he was still trying to figure out where to take her, Mose's wagon pulled up beside his. Trace looked up into his eyes. He wanted to tear into him for not letting him know what was going on, but in looking into his solemn brown eyes, so filled with sadness at seeing her like this, he knew that nothing needed to be said. He was sure that Giselle not telling him was what Mose had been angry about this morning. Mose had obviously wanted her to tell him, but she hadn't.

Even when he'd asked, she'd said she was fine. Why hadn't she trusted him? Was it a matter of trust or simply the best way she knew how to deal with a terrible situation? Knowing her, she was simply trying to handle things without being a burden to anyone else. He gently brushed a stray strand of hair out of her face, wishing that he'd been more attentive. She slept next to him every single night. He should have been close enough to her that she could trust him to help share some of her load. He should have been, but he wasn't.

Looking over at Mose, he got down to business. "I have to stop with her, Mose. She's going to bleed to death if we don't get her down and still." He sighed. "She may bleed to death anyway. Josiah said this has been going on for days. How much bedding have you got in your wagon? Are any of the blankets that we bought to take to California in yours?"

Mose tied off his reins on the brake handle and clamored into the back of his wagon and soon appeared with an armload of both blankets and sheets and a couple of feather pillows. They put their heads together to figure out if the VanKomen wagon had all the gear that he'd need to stay and help care for them without catching up to the wagon train to get more. Finally, they decided to move her to the back of Mose's wagon and go back to the rest of the train where they were nooning and get the gear that he would need. Then Mose would continue on with the train and their freight and Trace would try to catch up as soon as he could.

They were within just a few weeks of making it into the valley of the Great Salt Lake, but they might as well have been in Russia, as far as finding civilization nearby. A few weeks was a few weeks, and there was no short cutting the distance that they had to travel. The only place nearer than the Mormon settlement that was any settlement at all was Fort Bridger, and even it was a long, long way. Mose shifted a few things around and then Trace carefully lifted her across to the other wagon and they headed out.

The others were stopped only a mile or two ahead. Once they reached them, Trace went to talk briefly with John Sykes and then to his own wagon. Still wondering where he could stop to find any shelter, he worried about it out loud and Mose reminded him of a place not far ahead where there wasn't really shelter, but there was a cliff face that was undercut with a stream nearby. It wasn't ideal, but it would do. Tossing his own bedding and gear into Mose's wagon, he prepared to leave ahead of the others so that he could care for her as soon as possible.

As he went to leave, Mose handed him a couple of cold biscuits, and it reminded him of the biscuit that he had seen Mose give her that morning so long ago. "How long have you known, Mose? About the baby."

Giving his friend a sad smile, Mose said, "Do you remember how sick she was the morning after Filson was killed?" Trace nodded. "That's when I knew. She was so sick in the mornings. Just like Callie. I've been taking her biscuits every morning. If she ate before she got up, she wasn't so nauseated. But the deal was that she was supposed to tell you. She just never could."

"You've known this whole trip?" Trace felt more guilty than ever. "Why couldn't she tell me? Am I that scary?"

Shaking his head, Mose replied, "You weren't scary. Admitting to being attacked by a mob was what she couldn't face. I get the impression that she's tried to pretend that it never happened instead of dealing with it. When you get her healthy physically, you can tackle that one next. Someday she's going to have to face it."

Sadly, Trace said, "I'm a good doctor, Mose, but no one but God can fix some of the horrible things this world inflicts. You of all people should know that."

"You're right, Trace. But you'd be amazed what a strong husband can do in a good woman's life." He went to turn away and then stopped. "I'll be praying for you, friend. You and God are a majority in any struggle. But then you already know that."

When he reached the undercut, Trace fixed her a bed as far under the cliff face as possible. Then he began to set up a camp of sorts while he waited for her wagon with all the rest of her things to arrive. He started dinner and put hot water on to heat; both to clean her up with and to wash out her clothing as well. When the rest of the train made it to where he was, it was the work of only minutes to drop off the VanKomen wagon and take Mose's instead.

CHAPTER 8

As Trace watched the rest of the train leave without them, he had mixed feelings. He hated being left behind when time was so scarce, but he vowed here and now to take better care of Giselle. Granted, he hadn't known what delicate shape she was in, but he should have. He was a skilled physician. He should have realized what was going on.

In the last hour, he'd had to get honest with himself and admit that part of the problem had been that he cared about her so much that he had almost been avoiding her. That was backward, but it had been his way of protecting himself from getting even more attached to her when he knew that he was going to have to leave her behind in a few weeks.

That had been a good plan, but it had almost cost her life because he hadn't been close enough to see how weak and sick she had become. From here on out, he was going to take the best care of her whether it ripped his heart out later or not. Keeping his distance had been pure selfishness on his part.

After first checking on Josiah and Petja, he began to get Giselle cleaned up and changed. He needed to know exactly how much she was still bleeding to know how she was doing. Dressed only in her underclothing, it was obvious that she was expecting a baby. He had no idea how far along she was, but seeing that distinctive tummy brought his feeling of guilt one more time. Theirs hadn't been a real marriage in every sense, but he should have known. He should have known.

She didn't regain consciousness that day at all, and by that night as he and Dog sat up beside his fire, he finally had to let the past go. He hadn't meant to neglect her, but beating himself up mentally for not understanding would do no one any good. He had been praying for all of them all evening, and finally, as he lay down next to her and pulled her into a gentle embrace, he felt a sense of peace that, even if everything didn't work out the way he wanted, at least he could rest assured that God was in control here and was aware of them and their troubles.

Holding her now, he wished that he could apologize for all the mistakes he had made with her these past months. If he had known what she was going through he would have done so many things differently. Now all that he could do was to try to make things up to her as well as their circumstances would allow. That included being willing to be close enough to her to let her trust him, and to know what she needed without necessarily having to be told.

All night long he held her. She didn't ever wake up, and he was more than a little afraid that it was already too late and that she would die right there in his arms. When the sky began to lighten in the east, he got up and began doing all the things that needed doing to take care of three gravely ill people, as well as the mules and their cow and calf. When it was clear daylight, he fed Josiah and Petja as well as they could be fed in their illness. In looking for clothing for Giselle, he found a canvas bag that was filled to overflowing with blood soaked petticoats, and realizing anew how much blood she had lost, he became even more worried that she would never wake up.

He did more laundry and strung up a rope line to hang the clean clothes and then went to sit beside Giselle again. In the wagon, he'd found a book that he realized to be a journal of sorts that both Josiah and Petja had been keeping for a number of years. It began clear back when they were in Holland before they had even heard about the Mormon religion. He wondered if they would mind if he read it while he was here in camp, and in thinking about the kindly older couple, he didn't think they would care at all. Maybe it would give him some insight into why they had left their home and families and come here to this time and place. And maybe it would help him better understand Giselle and what she had been through.

They didn't write in it every day. In fact, there were times that they only wrote a time or two in a whole month. And then there were times that they wrote at length about what had been going on in their lives. He began to read and found that it was a fascinating tale of both heartache and a deep and strong love shared by the sweet couple.

After a couple of hours, he put the book aside to attend to Giselle and the others again and fix a noon meal. He'd fed Josiah and Petja and had eaten himself, when he heard the first sound out of Giselle in more than twenty-four hours. She moaned and sighed and turned onto her side, and it was the sweetest sound that he had ever heard. It was the first indication that she wasn't just fading away from him.

He didn't know if she could hear him or not, but he hoped that she could. There was so much that he wanted to tell her. Sitting down on the bed next to her, he tried to tell her how sorry he was that he had let her down and not understood what she had been going through this whole time. He told her to be strong and think positively so that she would heal and be able to move on with all the exciting things that God had planned for her life. He even told her how much he cared about her and how he wished that she had felt like she could talk to him about possibly losing this baby, and even being with child in the first place.

She didn't answer, but it helped him to be able to put some of his thoughts and feelings into words. It was something that he could do instead of just waiting and hoping, and it helped him to understand and to not feel like such a failure over all of this.

He was finally able to see that it wasn't all his fault like he had been feeling. She had been the one that had made a decision to hide her troubles from him even if it meant possibly risking her life. She probably hadn't even realized how dangerous losing this much blood could be. She had just been trying to make sure that she wasn't delaying their travel. He understood that now. He wished that she hadn't taken that much upon herself, but at least he could see that was what she had been thinking.

The hemorrhaging had slowed drastically from what it had been the day before, but it hadn't stopped altogether the way he had hoped. He had tried to hear a heartbeat for the baby with the sound horn that he had in his medical bag, but had no success. He assumed that, as bad as she'd been, she would indeed lose the baby, but the human body was a miraculous thing and you could never tell. So much had to do with the spirit and the individual will to live. He always felt like it was better to hope and work toward a miracle than to expect the worst.

All the rest of that day he alternated between caring for them and doing camp chores and reading in the journal. When she still hadn't awakened by the time he came to bed with her, he honestly doubted she would make it through the night this time. He knelt beside her to pour out his heart to God.

He told Him what was going on and how much he wanted these three people to be all right and be able to continue on to reach the place that they had struggled so hard to obtain. He told of how much he had come to care for this sweet and selfless woman, and about how frustrating it was to have spent so many years learning to help people medically but still not be able to do much right now to fix anything. He prayed like he hadn't prayed in a long time for divine help, and when he finally lay down, he still knew that things might not work out the way he wanted. But he also knew that God was watching over them and whatever happened here, it would be His will.

Even knowing that, if she died, it would be God's will didn't stop the heartache he felt. He agonized over any patient he lost, but he loved this particular one dearly and the thought of losing her was worse than he ever dreamed it would be. Facing losing her now made him wonder how he ever thought that he could honestly leave her in the Great Salt Lake Valley when the time came. He lay down next to her again and pulled her close, whispering, "Elley, please don't die. Please. I'd miss you so much. Stay here with me. We're going west, remember? To a wonderful new life for you. Stay with me, Elle. Please don't die."

He kissed her gently on the forehead and turned to look up at the stars. God was up there somewhere, looking down on them. "I know you can save her. Please leave her here with me. I'm trying to do as you would have me. Please. Don't take her yet. I need her."

After he said that, he realized how true it was. Always before he'd admired a pretty girl, enjoyed one's sense of humor, or even respected their talents or intelligence. But never until that day on the boardwalk in St. Joseph, Missouri had he felt the way he felt about this girl. He'd felt so strongly about her on sight, and then when he had realized she would be traveling with them, he honestly thought his feelings for her would fade when he got to know her better.

Just the opposite had been true. Her unique combination of beauty, strength of character, and sweet, happy way of serving those around her had made his emotions toward her stronger than ever. That was the exact reason that he'd felt obligated to keep his distance lately. It was almost a little frightening to need someone the way he needed her. What had frightened him even more was the thought of leaving her behind, but just now he wasn't sure that he'd even have her until they reached the leaving behind point. He'd deal with the whole leaving thing later. Right now, he'd settle for just knowing that she'd still be here beside him, alive in the morning.

In the first gray light of the predawn, as he came awake, he reached over and put his hand in front of her face and released a deep sigh of relief when he felt her breathe. She'd made it through the night. He felt the weight of his last night's fear slip away. She'd made it through the night and he was going to do whatever he could to see to it that she made it through a lot more. He pulled her tight to him again and thanked God for this gift.

There was frost on the blankets over them this morning. If he hadn't been so thrilled with just the fact that she hadn't died, he'd have been far more worried about those cold, little, white crystals. He lay there in their snug, warm cocoon, hoping that Josiah and Petja were warm enough as well. There was nothing that demanded urgency this morning, and he was content to stay here in bed and hold Giselle until the rising sun burned some of the chill out of the air.

His eyes were closed when she moved in his arms and he heard her softly say his name.

Pulling back to look at her, he thought he'd never seen anything more welcome than the clear, sky blue of her eyes. He looked into those sweet eyes and closed his to give a silent thank you for her life. Opening his again, he reached out and touched her cheek gently with one finger and softly said, "Good morning. Welcome back." The rush of emotion was hard to control. Finally, he was able to admit to her, "I was worried."

She hesitated and then said, "I've been worried too, Trace. There's something that I need to tell you."

He took her hand in his under the covers and laced his fingers through hers. "Elley, you don't have to tell me anything if you don't want to, but I already know about the baby. And it's okay. I mean, I don't know yet if the baby is okay, but you and I are okay, baby or no."

She looked away from his eyes. "I'm sorry that I didn't tell you."

Squeezing her hand gently, he admitted, "I'm sorry that you didn't too, Elley. I wish that I'd taken better care of you. And I wish that you would have felt like you dared tell me. I'm sorry that I've not been the kind of husband that you felt like you could tell. I'll do better, I promise."

She carefully shook her head. "It had nothing to do with the kind of husband you were, Trace. It's just a hard thing to deal with. But I am truly sorry. Please forgive me."

He pulled her close again and kissed her forehead. "Nothing to forgive, Elle. We're just going to keep on doing the best we can, and now that I do know, I'm going to do a lot of things differently. Will you forgive me for not taking good enough care of you?"

"Of course. It's not that you didn't take good enough care. If I'd realized how bad it was going to turn out, I'd have said something. I was just afraid that I'd delay the wagon train and we'd get caught in the snow in the mountains."

He turned and spoke into her hair. "I know. And I appreciate you trying to be strong for all of us, but I hope it hasn't come at the cost of your sweet, little baby."

She paused and then said, "I think there might be two. I always dream that there are two."

"You may be right. I just hope they're going to be okay. I have to be honest. The odds are that they won't survive what you've been going through."

He felt her sigh against his skin. "I know." After another minute she continued, "For the longest time I couldn't even think about them. Then Mose told me about his wife and her baby and how all babies need to be wanted and new life celebrated. I realized he was right, and I had finally resolved to love my twins." She swallowed hard. "Now I don't know what to think or how to feel. When I think about losing them, part of me wants to be relieved and part of me wants to cry forever."

He rubbed a hand over her back. "I can't say that I know how you feel, Elle, because I don't, but I know how I feel. I've only had a couple of days to think about this, and honestly, finding out that you had been harmed by a group of men rips my heart out.

"But I know that life is precious, and the babies certainly aren't to be blamed, although I'm sure that's hard for you. Mose was right, Giselle. New babies are one of God's greatest gifts of all. They do need to be loved and celebrated. In a perfect world, loving them in spite of all the circumstances would come easy. In reality, sometimes we humans are human.

"But I know you well enough to know that you are good and kind and Christian. No matter how this all works out, I know that you'll do the very best you can with whatever you are given. That's the kind of woman you are."

Looking up at him with those clear, bright eyes, she said, "Thank you, Trace. I hope that I'm worthy of your faith. Sometimes I think I am, and sometimes I think that I'll never have this follower of Christ thing down."

She leaned against him and he knew that talking was wearing her out. He rubbed across her back again and said, "God is watching over you, Elle. He'll help you handle this. For right now, all you need to worry about is resting and healing. Life will resolve itself one way or another." He pulled her head over against his chest. "Go back to sleep. Your body is weak. It needs some time, and worrying is not what the doctor prescribes. Just rest. We'll figure the rest of this deal out later." She laid her head down on his chest and was asleep again almost instantly.

He continued to hold her for almost an hour, pondering his life and what he wanted both in the near future and later. Never in his life had he been one to feel mixed up, but holding her now, he felt that way. Three months ago, he had a plan and had been happy knowing that he and Mose would be traveling to California again. He hadn't foreseen meeting Giselle and feeling this drawn to her. She'd thrown a kink into his careful organization.

The frost had long since burned off when he gently pushed her away and slid out of the blankets. He milked her cow and got breakfast ready and then fed Josiah and Petja. This morning he'd been encouraged by Giselle's finally waking, but her grandparents weren't doing better at all. Neither one of them was interested in food, and he could hear them trying to breathe through the rough membrane that was coating their airways.

He sighed as he climbed out of the back of the wagon and removed the handkerchief he'd been wearing over his face and washed his hands. Even as much as he knew about the human body, he longed for more understanding so that he could help them. They'd been down for weeks and looked like shells of the two robust people he had first met. He knew that the longer they were down, the weaker they would get, but as far as he knew, there was no miracle cure for what they had. Time would tell, he supposed.

Bringing food, he went again to Giselle. Although he was hesitant to wake her up, he needed to know how the bleeding was today. Sitting down beside her, he gently rubbed her back until she slowly opened her eyes to look up at him. In almost a whisper he said, "I'm sorry to wake you, Elle, but I need to check you. Please don't be offended. I need to know how much you've bled overnight."

She nodded and then closed her tired eyes again as he pulled back her bedding. He'd been hoping that with no movement the hemorrhaging would stop altogether, but he was disappointed. It was better than what it had been when he'd first found her, but she was still bleeding enough that she wasn't out of the woods. With the blood that she'd already lost, even the smallest amount was frighteningly dangerous.

At his sigh, she looked up at him again. "Bad?"

He nodded. "It's much better than it was, but you've lost far too much blood. How are you feeling? Are you cramping a lot?"

Tiredly, she shook her head. "Not too bad. Mostly I'm just tired and dizzy. Every once in a while the whole world starts to spin around me."

"How does food sound? Do you think you could eat something if I helped you?" She nodded again and went to sit up, but he stopped her. "No, Elle. Try not to move if you can help it. Moving will encourage the bleeding. If I give you bites, can you lie still?"

She made it through several bites before drifting off again while she was still chewing. He woke her and she managed to swallow, and then he let her go back to sleep.

When things were put to rights around camp, he climbed onto the cliff above them and looked all around. The Indians had been behaving for the most part as of late, and they were too far from the settlements to worry much about highwaymen, but being alone out here as they were was never that great of an idea. Even good Indians and settlers would be tempted by a lone wagon of ill people. When he saw nothing amiss around them, he went back to sit beside her and read in the journal some more.

It was an intriguing read that indeed helped him to gain insight into why the Mormons had gathered and why they were going west. He had heard stories about them, but had no idea how persecution had dogged them literally from the start. Even in their own country and among their own family they had been ill treated for the simple reason that they had chosen to believe that Joseph Smith had truly seen a vision back in eighteen-twenty. Trace closed the book around a finger that held his place and thought about that.

Told by the gossip mill that passed juicy stories along with an almost uncanny efficiency, the tale of the vision of God and Jesus Christ had seemed far-fetched and illogical, but here it made a kind of sense. Written in such a humble and straightforward manner that he could almost hear Josiah speak aloud, the idea that Christ's church had been lost from the world and needed to be restored in its original fullness rang true to something deep inside him. He tried to put himself in God's shoes. If the gospel had truly been lost to the earth, by what process could it be restored most correctly? Seen in that context, Joseph Smith's account only made sense.

He lost track of time reading until the light began to fade on the pages. He reached to touch Giselle's forehead with a gentle hand. She was cool to the touch and oh, so pale, but she was still with him. Setting the book aside, he pulled back her blankets to check her again and changed the toweling that he had put under her yet one more time. She didn't even wake as he did so, and he began to pray again as he worked around camp that night that she would pull through.

Josiah and Petja were worse, and when he finished doing all that he could do and then sat at the fire eating his own dinner with Dog at his feet, he began to wonder if all four of them were going to die on him. Or five, if she truly was carrying twins as she believed. It was a discouraging thought, and he finally went to sleep beside her with a heavy heart. In the night, he heard her groan and lit a lantern to check on her. She was in premature labor, and indeed before morning, she slipped stillborn twin girls.

She was bleeding heavily again, and as Trace wrapped the babies into a small blanket and set them aside, he continued to pray, knowing that he needed more than just his medical expertise to save her right now. When he came back to her, she opened her tired eyes and said, "If none of us make it, Trace, will you take the money to Brigham Young?"

He leaned closer, thinking that he hadn't heard right. "What was that, Elle?"

"The money in the bottom of the wagon. If none of us make it to the valley, will you deliver it?"

Wondering what she was talking about, he assured her, "You're going to make it, Giselle. You mustn't even question that, but you needn't worry about your money. We'll get it taken to Mr. Young." That seemed to calm her and she closed her eyes and went right back to sleep again.

At first light he started the regular day's chores and went to take care of Josiah and Petja. They were no better either, and the physician in him railed at the helplessness he felt. He couldn't get Petja to wake enough to eat and, as he fed Josiah, he asked how Giselle was. Trace felt like he had to be honest with him. "She delivered stillborn twins last night, and she's bleeding heavily. At this rate, she won't make it another day, Josiah. I'm sorry. In this primitive setting, there's nothing more I can do."

Josiah struggled to a sitting position. "Help me to her, Trace. I will bless her with God's power. She is meant to live. I'm sure of it. If she was supposed to die, she would have the night they attacked her. Help me to her."

Trace told him earnestly, "You'll need to wear a handkerchief over your face, Josiah. If she contracts what you have, she could never fight it off as weak as she is." Josiah nodded tiredly. Trace helped him cover his face, then lifted him out of the wagon, and carried the frail shell that was left of him to her under the cliff.

Seated on the bedding next to her, the old man gently placed his hands upon her head and proceeded to give a blessing in his native Dutch that was like nothing that Trace had ever witnessed in his life. His voice held a power that belied his present physical condition, and Trace could almost see Giselle gain strength under the feeble hands. When Josiah was finished, he was so weak that he slumped over onto his side, but his face shone as Trace lifted him to carry him back to the wagon.

Giving her the blessing seemed to take the last of his strength from him, and before the final rays of the sun slipped behind the western horizon, Josiah too had passed from this world. Trace went to lift his body out of the wagon and, as he did so, Petja opened sad eyes. "He's gone then?"

Sadly, Trace nodded. "I'm so sorry, Petja. He was a good man."

"That he was." Her mind seemed to wander for a second and then she said, "Please. Leave his body here with me for a while longer. I can feel his spirit still. He will be waiting for me. I must go to him soon, now that our work here is finished. You'll take care of Giselle for us?" He was unable to speak and nodded. "You're a choice young man, Trace. It has been good to have known you. Please tell her that we love her so. We will care for the babies for her."

Trace walked away from the wagon with a feeling of deep sadness, but there was something more. Petja talking about going with Josiah had been so matter-of-fact and peaceful. And how had she known about the babies? She had been completely unconscious when Trace had mentioned them, and he hadn't heard her and Josiah speaking since then.

He believed in a hereafter. What exactly it was like he wasn't sure, but he truly believed that life didn't end at the grave. But these people spoke of these things as if they had a sure knowledge, not only of what they needed to be doing here and now, but also of what they expected in the next estate.

He washed his hands and went back to check on Giselle before starting dinner, wondering if Petja had somehow known about the babies through an unseen power that he wasn't even aware of.

When he got to Giselle's bed under the cliff, she was wide awake and watching him in the dim light of dusk. He was surprised to find her so alert, but almost wished that she wasn't so he didn't have to tell her about her grandfather. Still emotional from talking with Petja, he uncovered her to check on her without saying anything. He wasn't able to see how much she had bled since the last time he had changed her toweling, and he covered her back up and went to bring a lantern.

Returning with the light, he pulled the linens back again and still found no blood. None at all. He was surprised and asked her, "Have you been up and changed these?"

Shaking her head, she said, "No. You told me not to move and I haven't."

Marveling, he pulled her blankets back up and tucked them around her. How had she gone from bleeding so heavily to nothing in a matter of minutes after Josiah's blessing? It didn't make sense medically and he shook his head, trying to find a logical reason that didn't include the obvious explanation that Josiah really had used God's power to heal her body. She noticed his expression and asked, "Is something wrong with me?"

Hesitating for a moment, he finally admitted, "No. Not at all, in fact. Your grandfather gave you this amazing blessing and you quit bleeding almost immediately. It... It seems like a miracle. I'm not sure what to think of it."

Smiling tiredly at him, she closed her eyes again. With them still closed, she said, "Christ performed a lot of miracles using the same power. Where is your faith?"

He looked at her and wondered that same thing for a moment. Knowing that he had to tell her, he said, "Giselle, I need to tell you something."

She opened her eyes again and looked at him almost serenely and he felt even worse about what he had to say. Before he figured out how to break the news to her, she asked, "Did my grandfather die?"

His eyes met hers and he nodded. "He did. I'm so sorry, Giselle. He loved you so much. Giving you your blessing was the last thing he did." He was watching her, wondering if he should tell her that her grandmother believed she was right behind him.

Tears quietly began to slip down her face, but her voice was peaceful when she replied. "He did love me. He was the only one that didn't think I was foolish to join the Church back in Europe. He and my grandmother. I almost hope that she goes as well. She'll be so lonely without him."

She tried to wipe her tears away with her hand and he handed her a handkerchief and admitted to her, "She believes that she's going to be going with him. I don't know what that means, but she was talking about it."

Giselle released the smallest of sighs. "I believe the veil is much thinner than most of us ever dream. Maybe she knows something that we don't. If she goes, I will miss her, but she'll be in a much better place. Someday, when there's another temple, I will have them sealed for all eternity. Theirs was a wonderful and true love. It would be a shame to end it at death."

Watching her talk about all this, Trace wanted to ask her a thousand questions about what she meant, but he didn't want to upset her further or tire her anymore. He sat with her for another minute until she closed her eyes again, and then he went to finish the evening chores and dinner. He fed Giselle before going to see to Petja, but he was unable to rouse the sweet, elderly woman to feed her. He lifted Josiah's body out of the wagon and prayed silently to himself for divine intervention to save both Petja and Giselle.

When morning finally came, Trace was grateful to know that Giselle hadn't hemorrhaged any more and, in fact, she was far more alert and clear-eyed than she had been since he'd found her collapsed on the wagon those days ago. His gratitude was short-lived though when he went to feed Petja and found that she too had departed this world during the night.

With a heavy heart he went back to tell Giselle and then began to dig a grave to bury them. As he dug, he tried to figure out how best to prevent Giselle from coming in contact with her grandparents and their belongings in hopes of preventing her from getting the same thing they had died from. Knowing that he could launder their bedding but not Josiah's oil skin slicker, Trace chose it to wrap their bodies in for burial.

With Giselle looking on from her bed, he gently placed the older couple and the tiny stillborn bodies in the grave and prayed over them before replacing the cold, gray earth over top of them again. He piled rocks on top and put a wooden marker with their names and the date burned into it. He could hear her crying softly as he did it, and when he was finally finished, he washed his hands again and came to her to gently stroke her hair.

Finally, he helped her sit up and held her for several more minutes as she cried. He knew that not only was she mourning their loss, but she now felt all but orphaned. He'd read enough of the diary to know that her family back in Holland had disowned her when she had joined the Mormons and that, other than her grandparents and himself as her husband of sorts, she was alone in the world.

At length, she even voiced what he knew she'd been thinking. "They were all the family that I had left. To my parents I am dead since I chose to join the Saints."

Determined to allay her fears, he reminded her, "You've got me, Elle. And soon you'll be back with the other Saints in Zion. Just a few more weeks."

She looked up into his eyes and didn't say it, but he knew that she was thinking that she didn't really have him. Theirs wasn't a real marriage no matter how much they both tended to ignore that fact. At times like this it was hard not to face the reality. He wanted so much to reassure her, but wasn't sure how to go about that.

Finally, he leaned and kissed her gently on the forehead. Maybe theirs wasn't a real marriage, but he wanted her to know that their friendship certainly was real. "Let's worry about the future later, Giselle. For now, I'm here and we're together and we're going to be all right. Today is a bad day, but we'll get through it."

He met her eyes steadily and finally he saw her decide to join him in taking one day at a time to make it through. He hugged her again, smoothed back her tousled hair and gently helped her lie back down. He brought her breakfast, sat with her while she ate, and then spent the day doing wash and getting ready to leave in the morning to try to catch up with the others. He carefully scrubbed anything that Josiah and Petja had been near and then rearranged the wagon to try to make a bed so that Giselle would be as comfortable as possible while they drove. He put all the bedding that he could under her in hopes of protecting her fragile body from the many jolts from the bumpy ride.

He planned to sleep in the wagon with her nights to share his body warmth now that the weather was so cold, and it was good that he did so because it began to rain that evening and they would both have been miserable trying to stay warm and dry apart. Holding her that night, listening to the rain on the canvas wagon cover, he knew that she was crying again and pulled her close. He didn't know how to help her get through this other than to make sure that she knew he was there for her.

Somehow, helping her helped him, but sometimes holding her body close to his was the hardest thing that he'd ever done. She was a beautiful, desirable girl and the only way being that close didn't make him crazy was to remind himself that she was his patient. Remembering how fragile her body was just now was the only way that he could keep from wanting more from her than just her body heat, and sometimes even knowing she was physically fragile didn't quite stop him from needing her.

When he woke up next to her in the early morning, he had to get up immediately and get right after the morning chores in order to keep his head straight. Then, when he went to help her down from the wagon so that she could refresh herself, she had to loosen the bodice of her dress to accommodate the fact that her milk had come in. He kept having to remind himself that he was her doctor and that she was obviously miserable so that he wouldn't think about how good she looked. He felt terrible for thinking about her that way, but he was far too human to be able to ignore her femininity.

On the way to milk the cow, he stopped by the stream to bathe in the frosty water in order to get himself under control, and then struggled to milk with hands that were stiff with cold. He grinned a self deprecating grin as he worked. This journey with just the two of them might be a lot more than he'd bargained for.

CHAPTER 9

They set out. Trace went at as fast a pace as possible knowing that they had four days to make up to catch the others. Not only that, but the others were already traveling as fast as possible and he was carrying a very fragile cargo. He glanced back at her through the wagon cover. Fragile and beautiful. Even deathly ill, she was exquisite lying there. How was he ever going to keep his distance?

Actually, it turned out to be easier than he thought it would be. Giselle was so weak that the only time they were together was when he brought her food or when they were lying beside each other at night. By then he was so tired from pushing hard from dawn to dark that it wasn't quite as difficult as he had assumed it would be. He tried to be up and moving by the time it started to get light and then drove until it was full dark before stopping.

For most of a week, Giselle lay still in the back of the wagon while he drove, but one morning he was surprised when she slowly climbed over the box to come and sit by him on the seat. She looked tired and drawn, and she only stayed for an hour or two before climbing back to lie down again, but from then on she spent more and more of each day sitting with him while he drove. By the time they were a little more than half way between Fort Laramie and South Pass, the famous gateway through the Rocky Mountains, she was spending several hours a day sitting there beside him.

Trace had known there was an Indian following them. He hadn't mentioned it to her, but it wasn't long before she figured it out. They didn't really openly discuss it, but they both began to be more diligent and careful. Dog was great about keeping them informed when the dark skinned prowler was around, and so far he didn't appear to be up to anything too sinister, but Trace knew enough about Indians to know that they were in for trouble. Trace assumed that the brave was simply biding his time, waiting for a chance to steal their stock or goods from the wagon. He didn't realize that it was his wife that he was after.

He figured that out fast one morning when Giselle was at the nearby stream washing her face while Trace hooked up the mules in the half light before dawn. Dog began to growl and, as Trace turned to investigate, he heard Giselle start to scream. She only got a split second of sound out before it was cut off abruptly and Trace and Dog both ran for the creek bank.

The Indian had her by the waist and his other hand was over her mouth as he attempted to drag her onto his horse with him. He'd have had her and been long gone except for the fact that Giselle was fighting him like a wildcat. Just as Trace reached the top of the bank, she must have bitten him, because the Indian winced and let go of her mouth, switched hands at her waist, and then hit her across the face with a closed fist.

The blow knocked her head back, but rather than settle her down, it only served to make her madder and she screamed again. This time it was in anger instead of fear, and she began to fight even harder. Trace could hear her cussing the brave out in her native Dutch as she fought with him. Dog tore into the Indian's horse and then latched onto the brave's foot as Trace reached them.

The Indian let go of Giselle to pull a knife on Trace as he kicked at the dog on the other side. Giselle lost her footing in the rocks when he let go so suddenly, and she almost fell under the horse's hooves. Instantaneously, Trace reached for her, throwing her away from the horse as he deftly deflected the brave's knife blade and pulled the man from the horse's back.

In a series of quick moves that felt like a death dance, Trace evaded the blade and moved further from Giselle before pulling his own knife from his boot. He heard Giselle gasp, and he glanced at her as the Indian brushed by him with his knife. He was grateful that she seemed to understand that he needed her to get back, and that Dog knew to stay with her as Trace focused once again on the desperate warrior in front of him.

Trace was taller and bigger and had the greater reach by far. That, coupled with the fact that he was more skilled with his blade, made for a short-lived fight. Literally within seconds, he had the Indian on his face with a knee in his back. The long, greasy, black hair tied with feathers was in his fist with the knife poised above the brave's brow. Trace struggled to control his anger. Normally slow to rile, seeing Giselle fighting for her life with this savage had made his blood boil instantly. A grown man treating a sweet, young woman like this made him furious! He almost wanted to run him through!

When he could finally speak without wanting to end it all right here and now, he told the brave angrily that he was a medicine man and that it would offend the Great Spirit for a medicine man to kill a warrior. He added that it would be the worst kind of bad medicine for the Indian to harm either Trace or Giselle, and that he was to leave them alone or Trace would call on the spirits to harm him. Still furious, the words literally ground out and Trace found it almost hard to speak the dialect.

When the Indian didn't respond, Trace shook him and let the knife draw a drop of blood. Still the brave didn't react, and Trace wondered if he was speaking the wrong language and tried a different dialect. Finally, the brave answered back in the first dialect in a voice full of anger, and Trace's fury raged through his veins again. He threw the Indian aside and gestured to Giselle and roared, "She is mine! Don't you dare come near her again! If you ever come back, I'll offend the Great Spirit and kill you anyway!" He waved the long bladed Bowie knife and kicked the brave soundly. "Get out of here before I change my mind!"

With a face devoid of expression, the Indian stood up, glanced at Giselle, and got on his horse and galloped away. Trace stood still for a moment, still battling his fury, trying to calm down enough that he wouldn't frighten Giselle any further when he went to her. He turned to her and searched her face for a moment before wrapping her in a hug. In a voice that was infinitely gentle, he asked, "Are you okay?"

She nodded against him and he continued, "I'm sorry I was so rough with you. I was afraid you were going to get stepped on." He pulled back from her and gently touched her face where the Indian had struck her. Her cheek was starting to swell and blood was crusting on the side of her mouth. "I'm so sorry, Elle. I should have been more careful. I didn't realize it was you he was after. I thought he would try to steal the mules, not you." He wrapped his arms back around her and rested her head on his shoulder. "I'm so sorry."

She started to cry and he hugged her tighter, wishing that he could undo the last ten minutes of her life. This probably brought back all the memories of the night she had been attacked by the mob. After several minutes of holding her tight and letting her cry, he took her hand and led her back to the wagon seat. They were loaded and ready to go and he helped her up onto the seat.

Climbing up beside her, he pulled her tight against him with one arm and snapped the reins to the mules with the other. "Let's get out of here, Elley. Let's get headed for home. Hopefully, we'll never see him again."

She sat tight against him for so long that his arm began to ache and she finally fell asleep there against him. She'd cried long enough that, even in her sleep, she breathed with little sobs from time to time. He was so sorry for her fear, but he had to smile when he thought back to the way she had fought the Indian. It wasn't fear that she had been feeling for a minute there. She had been telling that brave off with pure unadulterated anger at one point. And fighting! She probably would have been just fine on her own with him when she was so mad. It was only after everything was over that she had started to cry.

The thought of her at the hands of Filson and more like him made him want to be sick. What in the world possessed the hearts of men that they could harm a beautiful, sweet, young woman? He shook his head and pulled her tighter to his side. If he had known what had gone on, he would never have hesitated to shoot Filson. He still regretted that he hadn't done it and that he'd made her feel like she needed to.

He'd thought about it at length and realized that she had done it for him and the others in the train. If she had been going to do it to protect herself, she would have done it weeks and months earlier. No, she had done it to protect the others. He put a hand to her soft, blonde hair. She was an incredible woman.

Trace had told Giselle that he hoped they never saw the Indian again, but it didn't work out that way. The very next afternoon as they topped a ridge that dropped down into a thickly wooded stream bottom, they could hear something going on down in the brush near the creek. There was crashing around and growling and finally Trace heard what he knew was the unmistakable sound of a bear roaring and huffing. A couple of times they could hear the sound of a human voice and both bear and human sounds made the stock nervous.

Trace turned back around and pulled the wagon far enough away that the mules and cow and calf settled down, and then he tied the reins up and climbed down from the wagon seat with his rifle in hand. He turned to Giselle. "I'm going to see what's going on. I'm probably too late, but I have to know. Stay here with Dog. I'll be right back."

Twice before, he'd heard that sound of a bear, and both times he'd ended up with a severely mauled patient on his hands. The first one lived, although he would be hopelessly scarred for life. The second one didn't.

Carefully, Trace picked his way down through the trees until he could see what was going on below him. What he found made him glad that the sight of blood didn't bother him too much. It was the same Indian that had tried to steal Giselle the day before. He'd obviously come out on the worst end of an attack by a bear. The bear was still there, huffing and growling around, although it was dragging one hind leg and bleeding out of its nose and mouth. The Indian lay there in a gory pile, and at first Trace thought he was dead—until he saw the brave move to curl up into a ball when the bear approached him again.

When Trace realized the man was still alive, he raised his rifle and shot the wounded bear. On approaching the bear, he shot it one more time, just to be sure, and then he carefully approached the Indian. Somehow, the man was still conscious even though he was horribly chewed up. When Trace moved closer, he struggled to get away from him.

Trace looked all around and wondered where the man's horse was. He needed a way to carry the man up out of the creek bottom without injuring him further. Trace continued to look around and finally decided to carry the wounded man up the stream nearer to the ford to try to help him. Whether or not he could be saved remained to be seen, but Trace was going to give it his darndest. The physician in him would let him do no less.

Wondering how he was going to get the guy to let him work on him without a fight, Trace approached him again and was almost relieved to realize that the man was now unconscious. He carefully picked him up and carried him down to the stream crossing and laid him out beside it and then ran back up to Giselle and the wagon to bring them down as well.

Trace wasn't sure how to tell Giselle that he was going to try to save the man that had attempted to abduct her, but he knew that he couldn't just let him die without trying. He hoped she'd somehow understand. As it happened, she didn't even realize that it was the same Indian until Trace had him somewhat put back together.

On getting the wagon down, Trace went to work immediately cleaning the man up while Giselle started to build a fire and heat water without even being asked. The poor brave had been all but scalped by the bear, and the skin of his head hung in ragged strips of bloody, matted hair. His thigh was also torn up where the bear had apparently bitten him deeply and then dragged him or shaken him.

On top of that, he had cuts and puncture wounds in a myriad of other places, and it took Trace more than three hours to stitch him and put him back together as much as he could. He had to cut the man's hair off—and a good portion of the skin on his head as well—to try to save him. When Trace was finally finished, the Indian looked almost more frightening than when he'd started. With a tired sigh, he covered the wound on the Indian's thigh with the final bandage. Honestly, if this man lived, it would be surprising. He was incredibly torn up and wounds like this tended to fester horribly.

It was late afternoon when he finally washed his hands again and looked up and met Giselle's eyes. She had helped him all the way through the surgery without faltering, and he was unbelievably proud of her—both for how competent a helper she was and for continuing to help even when she figured out that it was the same Indian. She began to clean up and Trace said, "We'll need to move on before we camp. The dead bear and all the blood will attract other predators, so we'll move on up the trail before stopping."

She nodded at him and he went and skinned the bear. There was no sense in wasting the hide, even though as he skinned it he found that the Indian had put up quite a fight. There were several punctures and bullet holes in the hide. Trace was sure that the bear would have eventually died of the wounds.

On an impulse, Trace also saved its teeth and claws. He was going to assume that his patient would make it and he would want these sometime. Trace cut out as much of the bear meat as he thought they could use before it spoiled and took it back to the wagon. He wasn't sure where to put the Indian. Giselle had been wonderful about helping to save his life, but Trace didn't want to traumatize her any more than was necessary. Finally, he rigged up a travois, attached it to the back of the wagon with two dead trees and a sheet of canvas, then gently laid the still-unconscious man on it, and they pulled out.

It was full dark when they finally stopped for the night a few miles up the trail, next to the same creek where he'd rescued the Indian. They built a cook fire and started dinner. After being so roughly handled the day before, Giselle had started to hemorrhage again. When she automatically started helping, Trace thanked her kindly—and then just as kindly, but firmly, sent her to lie down in the back of the wagon. She hardly even argued, and he knew that she was tired and worried as well.

He cooked and did the camp chores and tended to his patient. When he finally made it to bed with her, he was tired, even though they hadn't traveled all that far that day. He lay down next to her and pulled her close to him. She stirred in her sleep and patted his hand gently and said something in Dutch before she rolled close to him and settled back. He had no idea what she'd just said, but somehow he knew that she'd just told him that she was proud of him. It was the tone of her voice and the way she'd touched him, and it made him even more grateful to have her around. She always made him feel good about himself.

Twice in the night he got up to check on the Indian, and both times he wondered if they would find him still among the living when morning came. He was grievously wounded and Trace wished for the power that Josiah had blessed Giselle with. It had been so much stronger than his medical skills that day.

As he lay there beside her, waiting to get back to sleep, he thought about that priesthood and her church. Since they had been traveling, he hadn't had a chance to read any more of the journal and he found that he truly missed it. Sometimes while he drove, she read a book that he had come to realize was the Book of Mormon. He didn't know much about it except that some people referred to it as the Mormon Bible, but she seemed to cherish it and he wished sometimes that she would read it aloud to him. He would have already asked her except that he knew it would tire her.

When he woke up beside her the next morning, he lay there enjoying her warmth for a few minutes until he had to get up and away from her to keep from wanting more. He had come to realize that it was a fine line he was walking, between caring for her and caring too much for her. Unless he was dead tired, being that close to her was the hardest thing he'd ever tried to do. It made for a lot of mornings where he had to get right up and get busy or he'd have gone crazy.

As he stood at the end of the wagon and pulled his shirt on, he watched her sleep. She never seemed to struggle with sleeping beside him at all. He must not be as incredibly tempting to her as she was to him. He turned to check on his other patient with a wry smile on his face at the thought. That was probably a good thing. Both of them fighting this for each other would have been impossible.

The Indian had made it through the night, although he was feverish and swollen beyond recognition this morning. Sometime in the night his horse had found him and was standing there with its head hanging over him when Trace came around the wagon. At first it spooked off a little, but eventually it let him catch it. Trace moved the travois to the horse instead of the wagon for fear the Indian would get stepped on with three animals tied to the wagon next to him. Trace cared for his wounds, got breakfast, did chores, and they pulled out without the Indian ever stirring in the slightest. Today would be the day that they learned if he would make it or not. Trace wished again for that higher power.

When Giselle climbed out of the wagon box to sit beside him on the seat after an hour or so on the trail, he looked over at her with concern. "Are you sure you should be up today, Elle? Are you still bleeding?"

She leaned her head against his shoulder and laughed a little self consciously. "You always ask me the most embarrassing questions, Tracey. I guess I should be used to you by now, but you still make me blush. Yes, I'm still bleeding a little, but do I have to be stuck in the back of the wagon? Can I sit here with you for even a few minutes?"

He chuckled at her and said, "Sorry. But you married a doctor. It's what I do. I can't change it. Blood isn't really optional. I nearly lost you and don't want to take chances again. Ya' know?"

She put her hand on his thigh. "I'm sorry for everything, Trace. And I'm unbelievably grateful that you're a doctor. When I watch you work, it amazes me. I'm so proud of you. I'm just still a little shy sometimes is all. But I'm the very first to acknowledge that you saved my life."

He thought about that for a minute and then admitted to her, "But I didn't, Elley. You were so out of it that you didn't know, but I think if it had just been up to my medical skills you would have died. I was doing the best I could, but you were still fading on me. It was Josiah that saved your life."

He looked at her honestly. "I hate to even admit that, but it's true. If he hadn't been able to get the bleeding stopped, I'm afraid I would have lost all five of you. That was my worst day of being a doctor ever. Four died and the fifth would have." He shook his head sadly. "I miss your grandparents. And I only knew them for a short time. I'm sure it's much harder for you. They were remarkable people."

A single tear escaped her eye and rolled slowly down her cheek. "I miss them too. I always try to remind myself that they're in a wonderful place."

He drove for a few minutes and then asked her, "How do you know so surely where they're at, Giselle?"

He could feel her looking up at him before she answered. "Our Father in Heaven reveals the things that we need through His prophets, Trace. He knows that we need to understand His plan for us. He has always spoken through his prophets, and now He does again.

"I know that sounds strange. I didn't believe that there was a prophet again at first, but now I know that there is. It's the most comforting thing I've ever experienced. The prophet here on earth is the greatest of all gifts. Knowing God's will, without doubting, is incredibly precious to me."

He glanced down at her. How would it be to feel as sure about eternal principles as she did? There was such a sweet, calm intensity about her sometimes that it left little to question. Her knowledge came across with such a sense of sureness. He didn't doubt her when she was like this. It would have been impossible. Her honesty and faith carried a spirit of its own.

He had more education than most people the world over, but that was nothing compared to her faith. He'd have gladly traded his years of learning for her knowledge about God. He decided that it was time he understood some things like she did. "Tell me about the power that Josiah used when he blessed you. What do you have to do to have it?"

"The power that my grandfather used is God's power, the same power that Christ used when he walked the earth back in biblical times. Grandfather held the Melchizedek Priesthood. He received it from another priesthood holder that had the authority to give it to him. Men that are baptized members of The Church of Jesus Christ of Latter-day Saints, and are worthy, can hold the priesthood and administer priesthood ordinances using it. It's the exact same organization, using the same power as Christ's original church organization with the first twelve apostles like Peter, James and John."

He had to question that. "How could it be the same power? Wouldn't that original authority have been lost after this many years? That was more than eighteen hundred years ago."

Nodding her head, she agreed with him. "That's why it all had to be restored."

He remembered reading in Josiah's journal about how the original church was restored, but he hadn't equated that with original power and authority. He thought about all these things as he drove with her sitting quietly beside him. He got so involved with his thoughts that he didn't even think to encourage her to lie back down before they stopped for their nooning. When he helped her down from the wagon seat, he noticed the blood on her dress, but didn't say anything. He didn't want to embarrass her, but after she had eaten, he was insistent that she stay lying flat for the rest of the day.

His Indian patient didn't regain consciousness that whole long day as they traveled, and when Trace bedded the camp down that night, he was discouraged, thinking that the man probably wouldn't make it through the night as rough a shape as he was in. When Trace climbed in next to Giselle, she was awake and picked right up on his discouragement. When he explained, she put a gentle hand on his chest as she lay beside him. "You've done your best, Trace. Let's give it over to God now and trust that He will do as he sees fit with this man. God is in control and He can do anything. Will you pray with me?"

He covered her folded hands with his and she prayed simply and fervently that the Indian would be healed if it be God's will. When she ended her prayer, she patted him gently again, laid her head on his chest, and got so quiet that he thought she had gone right to sleep. With her this close, sleep for him was decidedly elusive. In fact, if she hadn't been lying right on him, he probably would have gotten clear up and gone back out to the fire.

As it was, he lay there, struggling to think of something other than how good she felt and how wonderful she smelled. When she spoke to him again more than a half hour later, he was surprised. He'd thought she was long asleep. Her sweet voice and her breath on his skin did nothing to allay his struggle. "Trace? Are you still awake?"

He put a hand on her shoulder. "Yeah. Why?"

"I just wondered. I'm awake too. I can't sleep for some reason tonight."

He chuckled at her softly. She seemed honestly perplexed about that. He wasn't perplexed. He knew exactly why he couldn't sleep.

CHAPTER 10

That night they heard wolves again for the first time in weeks, and she rolled over tight against him. She seemed to go right back to sleep again, but he wasn't that lucky. For the second time that night he tried to focus on anything but her.

It had taken him long enough to drop off to sleep both times that night that he was still tired in the morning, and probably would have still been in bed at sunup if he hadn't heard Dog growl. He got up and slipped out of the wagon to see what was going on. He was pleasantly surprised, actually. Dog was growling at the Indian.

He was awake-if you could call it that. His eyes were as open as he could get them, as swollen as his face was, and even though he was still feverish, his eyes were clear and he was with it enough to be afraid when Trace came to check on him. Trace could tell that he had no idea what to think when Trace approached him to touch his forehead to feel how hot he was.

Trace said good morning to him in his own language before moving his blankets to check the bandages on his thigh. All of the other injuries seemed to be doing okay, but the thigh still looked ugly and inflamed. Trace wondered if he was going to have to open it back up to let it drain. The brave's eyes widened when he saw the rows of stitches that criss crossed the large muscle of his upper leg, and he looked up at Trace in surprise. Trace chuckled at the man that had remained so stoic the other day during their altercation. "I told you I was a medicine man."

He reached for a leather pouch that he had tied to the travois beside the man's head and handed it to him. It contained the bear's teeth and claws that Trace had saved for him. "You killed the bear, but it almost got you in the mix of things. I saved the hide too, but you're going to have to bargain with me for it." The Indian looked up and met Trace's eyes as he checked his other wounds for infection. "You're going to live. Lie still and behave yourself and I'll bring you something to eat."

Giselle must have heard him talking, because she leaned up and poked her head out of the canvas wagon cover. Trace looked up at her and smiled. Then to the Indian he said in a no nonsense voice, "She's *mine* Great Bear Killer. Stay away from her! Or I'll undo everything that I did." He nodded at the stitched wounds and gave the brave a stern look. The Indian glanced up at Giselle and back at Trace and nodded, then closed his eyes.

Trace looked up at Giselle again. Even just waking up she was exquisite. It was no wonder the brave had wanted to steal her. He ran a hand through his hair and turned to start camp chores. He had to get a handle on this physical attraction thing. He still had a long way to go traveling with her. It was going to take all of his self control just to get her to the valley of the Great Salt Lake, let alone leaving her there when they made it.

When he took her breakfast, she asked him what he had said to the Indian and he tried not to look too guilty when he told her. "I said that you were mine and he was to leave you alone or I'd undo it all. Hopefully he knows by now that I mean it. If he bothers you, I'll finish what the bear started."

Her eyes got wide. "Don't worry. Indians are usually wildly superstitious. I'll bet that he thinks I'm relatively mystical after the way he's patched together. I doubt he would dare bother you again. But don't tempt him, just to be safe. There's no such thing as a native women that looks and smells as good as you. Your medicine may be more powerful than mine." Her eyes got even wider and he chuckled at her as he walked away.

The night after the Indian woke up, they heard wolves again, and this time they ended up coming right into camp. Trace heard Dog growl and start to snarl, but before he made it out of the wagon, the wolves had attacked the calf. Trace shot one of the wolves and saved the calf, but the next morning, before they headed out, he had to patch it up, too. Giselle helped him again, and as the calf limped away, he remarked, "She'll never race, but she'll make a great milk cow if we can get her all the way to Zion without the wolves catching her again."

For two days the brave dragged along behind them in his travois, hardly even looking up. He was still gravely ill and slept almost constantly. The second morning, Trace determined that he needed to reopen the wound on his thigh to see if he could drain some of the infection. Even as well as he seemed to be doing, Trace knew he would not make it if he couldn't get that big wound to clear up. He went to him and asked the Indian his name to which he replied, "Many Feathers." At that, Trace got into the wagon and borrowed Giselle's hand mirror and brought it out to him.

He showed the brave the mirror and said, "I'm sorry, but I had to cut off Many Feathers' feathers." When the Indian saw his image, his eyes widened until he almost looked panicked for a moment. He lifted a hand to feel the patchwork of stitches and closely cropped hair mingled with the almost black patches of scabbed-over skinless flesh. He shuddered uncontrollably and looked up at Trace in open fear for a moment before his stoic mask fell back into place. Trace tried to reassure him. "I'm a powerful medicine man, Many Feathers, but your leg doesn't heal. I need to do more work on it."

The Indian nodded and Trace went on. "It will be very painful. I need to put you to sleep to do it."

At this, Many Feathers shook his head and thumped himself on the chest with a fist. Helping him to understand what Trace intended was pointless. Many Feathers had no experience with Trace's ether and couldn't be expected to trust what Trace was trying to tell him. At length Trace decided to just try to do it with him awake. Who knows? The Indians he had known were incredibly tough people. Maybe this man could take it.

Trace went and got Giselle to come and help him. When she came near she acted fine, although she wouldn't look right at Many Feathers; but her hands shook when she handed Trace his instruments. Still, she willingly stood by to assist him and he had to respect her strength.

As Trace made the initial cut into Many Feathers' leg, the Indian made a gasp in spite of himself, and his already sickly pallor went an almost gray white. Gooey, smelly, yellow pus streamed out of the wound, and Giselle closed her eyes and then made a dive for a nearby bush and lost her breakfast. She wiped her face on the hem of her petticoat and after sitting still for a minute and taking several deep breaths, she came right back to Trace's side to finish helping him.

Trace drained the wound and cleaned it out again, and this time left it open so that it would continue to drain on its own. He cleaned up the mess and rebandaged it. When he was finished, Many Feathers' lips were a tense blue line and his skin was ghostly between the scabbed-over cuts. Trace finished and spoke to him apologetically, wishing that he at least had some whiskey to give the poor man, as terrible as that sounded.

Every time that Trace checked on him that day, he knew that he wasn't sleeping and assumed it was because of the pain, but the wound in his thigh became markedly less inflamed within just a couple of hours and, by that evening, he appeared to be out of the woods for good. The next morning Many Feathers struggled to his feet and dragged himself into the bushes beside the stream near their camp. When he came back a few minutes later and lay back down on his travois, Trace knew that he was eventually going to be all right after all.

It was a marvelous feeling to know that you had helped another human being to stay alive. Giselle came up to him as he watched Many Feathers settle back onto the travois, and she put her arm around Trace's waist and hugged him. With a huge smile, she patted his chest and said, "Wonderful job, Medicine Man Grayson. You are a fine physician, not to mention a very handsome one. He will heal beautifully. I'm sure of it!"

She hugged him again and went off toward the wagon to lie back down and Trace watched her go, wondering what he was going to do about her. He didn't think he could stand to leave her behind. He looked up to find Many Feathers watching him with deep, dark eyes. When Many Feathers glanced back up at the wagon, Trace reminded him gruffly, "She's mine! Don't even look at her!"

That night, Many Feathers approached him soberly and, in an absolutely friendly manner, offered Trace three blankets for Giselle. Trace was horrified, but tried not to let it show on his face as he calmly turned him down. Many Feathers stayed with them one more day and night. Finally, Trace told him that he believed that he would be okay and when Many Feathers said that he needed to return to his home soon, Trace explained how to cut out the stitches in several more days and how to care for his wounds until they healed.

Before Many Feathers rode away on the ninth day, he offered Trace the three blankets as well as his horse for Giselle. Trace turned him down flat again and Many Feathers looked up at the wagon and then turned and rode off. Trace smiled to himself to realize that he was actually going to miss the man.

Even traveling from before it was light until full dark every day except when they had found Many Feathers, they still hadn't caught up with the rest of the train. Honestly, Trace didn't even think they were close. All sign of the other wagons was several days old at every camp.

Giselle was doing better, but she was so weak, and though she spent part of every day sitting with him, she still lay in the back of the wagon a good portion of the time. When she sat with him, she would answer his questions about her church as they drove and he'd finally asked her if she would read to him from her book. He wasn't sure if it was intriguing to him because of its content or because of the fascinatingly sweet voice and accent that she read to him with. Maybe it was both. Her reading was hypnotic, but the story line was fantastic. Whatever it was, he was becoming enthralled with the book and looked forward to those hours that she read aloud to him as they traveled.

Just a few days after Many Feathers rode away, he came back one morning. He came to Giselle and left her a leather bag full of pine nuts and then approached Trace. This time, he offered two horses and a prime buffalo hide. It was a beautiful hide, but still Trace didn't even glance at it before he turned the offer down. Many Feathers looked longingly at Giselle and then rode away again.

Giselle asked him right out if Many Feathers was trying to buy her. Trace wasn't sure how she had figured it out, but he had to level with her. When he admitted that he was, she wanted to know how long this had been going on. With a guilty smile, Trace admitted, "Since a couple days after the bear."

Giselle was mad clean through, Trace tried to mollify her by explaining that it was simply the way Indians did things. She didn't mollify very easily, and she was still mad when they stopped for the evening. When he lay down next to her and put an arm over her, she turned to him and tried to apologize for being angry. He laughed softly at her and gently pulled her close to pray with her. At least she was mad and not scared over the whole thing.

For some reason, when Many Feathers was well enough to leave them, a lot of things started going wrong all at the same time. It wasn't just that the weather turned cold and blustery. The wolves dogged them, and between the intermittent rain and sometimes even snow, the trail got sloppy. Then they had the first major wagon breakdown that they'd had the whole trip. Trace spent most of one afternoon repairing a wagon wheel that had begun to wobble.

That evening when Many Feathers showed up again, Trace was glad to see him and enlisted his help in taking the whole wheel off and then putting it back on after he'd finished repairing it. Giselle disappeared into the wagon as soon as Many

Feathers appeared and wouldn't come out even when he wanted to present her with a quarter of venison. Before he left, he offered Trace three horses and a finely tanned set of buckskins.

That night as they lay down, Trace teased her about how tempting those buckskins had been. She leaned up on one elbow and asked him, "You wouldn't really sell me, would you Trace?"

He laughed and pulled her back down to lie against him. "No, Elley. I would never sell you. Go to sleep." After a few seconds he said, "Well, maybe. If he ever offered ten horses. But I've never heard of anyone ever offering that much, so you're probably safe."

She smacked him in the dark and for the first time, they got into a little wrestling match there in the wagon and ended up laughing together until Trace finally got the upper hand. He got hold of both of her arms and as he leaned over her there in the moonlight, he looked down at her and the smile died out of his face. He looked down at her and she looked up at him and somehow they were no longer laughing.

He wanted to kiss her so bad that he could almost taste it, and before he even realized that he was doing it, he did. Just once. It was gentle and relatively fast and she tasted like heaven, but it took both of them by surprise. She looked up at him with big, quiet eyes in the darkness and he sighed and lay down next to her, feeling incredibly guilty about both kissing her and still wanting to do it again.

He groaned and tried to apologize. "Sorry, Elle. I didn't mean to do that, I swear. I don't know what got into me." He put an arm around her shoulders and pulled her close. In a truly penitent voice, he said it again. "Sorry."

The wagon was quiet for a few seconds, and then she laughed softly and leaned up and smiled and said with her distinctive accent, "It is okay. We are friends. We *are* married- at least for a while. You have saved my life a number of times, and I love you dearly. It is okay. It was nice. But we should be careful, because soon we will have to leave each other, and you would break my heart into a thousand pieces if you did it often.

129

We have been through enough things to deal with this. No? Kissing me on accident I can handle. Just do not sell me." She laughed again and threatened as she lay back down, "I would have a very hard time forgiving you." She snuggled over to him and sighed.

After another minute or two, he admitted, "It's not you handling it that I worry about, Elley. I have to be honest with you and tell you that sometimes it's incredibly hard to lie here by you and not want to do things like kiss you. There are times that you are far too tempting. Sometimes I've felt so guilty because I even felt that way when you've been so sick. It makes me wonder what kind of a doctor I am that I sometimes want to be close to my patient. Like really close."

She leaned over and laid her head on his chest and rested her hand on him as well. "Ours has been an interesting trail west, hasn't it Trace? I know what you mean about lying beside each other. There are times it has been so hard to remember that we're not really married. But can I tell you that sleeping beside you has also been the sweetest peace I have ever known? When we started this trip, I was so incredibly afraid. I can't even tell you. I can't even explain that fear. I wouldn't even want to try.

"And then even when Filson was gone, I had never slept outside before. And the wolves and the storms and all the things like Indians and robbers. But I've always known that I was safe here beside you, even when everything was strange and different, and even when I didn't really know you that well. I've always known that you would watch over me.

"Then when I thought that I was dying, even then, I knew that whatever happened, it would all be okay because you were here. That has been the most priceless gift to me. Someday, in a few weeks when I have to tell you goodbye and pray that you get to California safely…"

She sighed. "I'm going to miss you more than you will ever know, Trace, but 'til the day that I die, I will always be grateful for being able to lie here beside you and know that I'm safe with you. My heart will be broken, but I will always love you and be so thankful for you. You have been the sweetest and best friend and protector for me. Thank you.

"I only wish there was some way to return this gift. There isn't and I know that. How could I ever repay a gift this great? It can't be done. But please know how much I appreciate you and all you do for me." She leaned up and looked at him and then gently kissed him one more time. She laid her head back down on his chest. "I do love you, Trace. I'm sure I always will."

He wrapped his arm around her again and played with a strand of her silky hair. "I love you too, Elley. Good night."

Long after she finally fell asleep, he lay there thinking about her and what she had just said. Her sweet honesty had been both wonderful and terrible. It had been heaven to hear her tell him her innermost thoughts and feelings, and he didn't doubt them for a second. He was sure that she did love him. It was just hard to hear her say that and, in the same breath, talk about how they would be leaving each other and that she was okay with that.

He knew that was still the plan, but he wasn't okay with it at all. He really, really wasn't okay with it. He never wanted to leave her for the rest of forever and ever. He didn't just love her now after these last months. He was in love with her and couldn't for the life of him honestly picture himself walking away when the time came.

CHAPTER 11

It snowed that night. Real snow that stuck to the ground and settled on top of the ice in the water bucket. The next morning the world was beautiful with its pristine dusting, but both of them looked at the low, ragged gray clouds with concern. By that afternoon it had all melted off again; and the clouds blew away and they had a trouble-free day for once, but it was a rude reminder of what they could be up against. They pushed ahead hard and didn't stop until it was too dark to see where they were going. They made dinner in the cold and dropped into bed too exhausted to even worry about wanting to hold each other.

They had several more good days of travel in a row. The freezing temperatures actually helped in a way, because the trail was good and solid until after mid-day when the October sun finally thawed the mud out. On those cold nights they were incredibly grateful for each other's warmth.

Every few days Many Feathers would appear to up the ante for Giselle. He had followed them for nearly two hundred miles across an expanse of the Wyoming territory. Trace had been relatively sure that once they hit Fort Bridger, he would turn back and head for his own home, wherever that was, but just one day after they left the fort, he showed up early in the morning and indeed offered Trace ten horses for her. He left her a beautiful elk hide tanned with the hair on, even though Trace had turned down his offer as usual.

Once he was good and gone, Giselle came out of the wagon and stretched her hands out to the warmth of the breakfast fire. Trace came up behind her and wrapped both arms around her and said with a laugh, "Well, you're up to ten horses." He laughed again and she turned to him with unbelieving eyes.

"Really? Ten horses?"

He nodded with a grin. "Ten horses. That's got to be some kind of a record!"

She leaned down to stir the breakfast porridge. "Ten horses. Buying wives is barbaric, but that's a lot of horses!" He turned to finish hitching up the mules and she asked, "You're sure you wouldn't sell me?" He laughed all the way to the team.

They had passed Fort Bridger on the eighteenth of October and it had been the perfect Indian summer day, but then the weather turned cold with a vengeance. At least it was cold and dry for a couple of days. Finally, one morning they were slogging along in wind driven sleet that froze onto anything that it touched. They were wending their way through the part of the trail that wound in and out of the Bear River Valley, and of course the rogue mule chose that day to act up again.

Before they were even under way that morning, the trail and everything near it was covered with a grainy coating of ice. By the third time they had to cross the river, the mule was positively balking, and every time they hit an ice covered rock, it would simply stop and stand in the harness with its huge ears pinned back against its head. Several times Trace had to ask Giselle to come hold the reins for him while he rolled rocks out of the way or levered a wheel out of a bind. Finally, Giselle just insisted that she drive while he walked along beside the wagon so that they didn't have to keep starting and stopping.

At first Trace wanted to argue with her, but then he looked around and realized that, if they didn't make headway soon, they were going to be camped in the middle of the very river bottom. If things got any worse, they'd never get out the next morning after more ice or snow.

Even with Giselle taking the lines and him clearing the way and pushing, they didn't make it up out of the bottoms until long after dark. Parking the wagon as far under the lee of a hill as he could get it, Trace sent Giselle to go get out of her wet clothes while he unhitched the team and got the stock into some shelter as well. She had been driving today in just her dress and two heavy shawls that she had wrapped around her. The shawls had long since soaked through and she was wet to the skin. He would have given her his own slicker except that it would have drowned her, and he knew that she would never have taken it anyway when she had the protection of the wagon cover from time to time.

It took him forever to unhitch and move the stock into the scant shelter of the hill, and the mule balked even when all he was trying to do was give it a bait of grain to augment the meager feed nearby. By the time Trace finally headed to the wagon, he decided they were going to have to make do with cold leftover bread and meat for dinner, because it would have taken all night just to get a fire started in this mess. He climbed into the back of the wagon and paused to take off his streaming slicker, wondering why Giselle hadn't lit the lantern yet. He had his slicker off and was starting on his boots when he realized that she wasn't even in the wagon at all. He leaned out of the flaps to look around and see where she had gone. He couldn't see a thing in the dark and the storm, and hurried to pull his slicker back on so that he could help her get back in and dry as soon as possible.

Walking through the sleet and the rain, he called her name repeatedly and had just begun to truly worry, when he literally tripped over her in the dark. She was sitting on the ground just beside the wagon wheel that she usually used to climb into the wagon, and she had her knees drawn up and her arms wrapped around them and was fast asleep. When he touched her, he was horrified to realize that she actually had a layer of ice on her head. It shattered under his hand, and without even bothering to try to rouse her, he picked her up and laid her on the wagon seat and began to undress her so fast that he accidentally ripped some of her buttons off in his haste.

Giselle was cold, far too cold, and the fact that she didn't even respond to being picked up and undressed scared him. She was still so weak from the loss of blood that it wouldn't take much for her to freeze to death like this. When she was free of her dress and petticoats, he set her inside the wagon box, climbed in beside her, and removed her boots and stockings as well. He put her in the bed and hurried to take off his dripping slicker and boots and rooted around for a towel.

As he was rubbing her hair and skin with the towel to try to get her blood moving again, she finally roused enough to moan and try to move away from his brisk treatment. She opened her eyes and looked up at him sleepily and said, "I'm cold, Trace. Will you hold me?"

He pulled her head against his chest for just a moment and answered under his breath, "Yes, I'll hold you, Elley. Stay with me, girl. And please forgive me in the morning, but we've got to get you warm." She was well on her way to freezing to death, and there wasn't a thing he could do about it except warm her up with his own body heat on this frigid, wet night. At this point, he was grateful that he'd had to do so much physical labor. Dry under his slicker as he'd been, the struggle had kept him warm even in the bitter cold, and that warmth was the only thing that was going to save her life tonight.

He stripped off his own gear down to his long underwear and climbed beneath the quilts with her. Her cotton underclothes were soaking as well, and in frustration, he removed them, working as fast as he could, and then wrapped his whole body around her to try to share his warmth. She was so cold that she wasn't even shivering, and swearing in his concern for her, he sat up and pulled off his long handles too and gathered her back into his arms.

He could finally feel how frighteningly cold she was, and he wondered if he was already too late. Her hands and feet were like ice and he hesitated to even rub them for fear of injuring them if they had already frozen. He pulled the blankets up over their heads and wrapped his body around hers as well as he could and tried to get her to wake up. He was afraid that she would simply go to sleep and die on him.

After what seemed like hours, Giselle finally began to shiver and her teeth began to chatter together painfully hard. Now he was thoroughly chilled through too, just from trying to warm her, and his teeth chattered as well. She woke up enough to talk to him, and she began to cry into his chest as she shivered. She kept trying to pull her hands away, and he knew that they were beginning to tingle and hurt miserably as the blood began to move through them again. He hugged her to him gently and tried to talk to her to explain that she needed to stop fighting him and help him warm her, but it was a long time before she finally understood and lay still, sobbing quietly against him.

It was deep into the night before he felt like she was actually more warm than cool against him. He still rubbed her gently and moved his legs around hers to warm her on all sides, while he slowly and carefully rubbed her hands and arms to try to get warmth to them.

He felt like he'd been at this for an eternity when she sighed against him and whispered, "Thank you, Trace. For saving me again. Isn't it nice not to have to wrestle with all those clothes for once? Tonight is the first time I don't feel like a *flanel bord geschiedenis*." She turned onto her side and snuggled against him like a set of spoons, gently sighed one more time and went to sleep.

For the first time that night he was comfortable with letting her rest. The storm outside raged against the canvas wagon cover, and now that they were safely inside and warm and dry, it was almost a comforting sound. It made the wagon and their nest of thick quilts feel like a cocoon again, insulated from the rest of the world around them. He sighed as well, pulled her tight into his arms, and let his own completely exhausted body drift off, wondering what in the world a *flanel bord geschiedenis* was.

When he woke up the next morning, the storm had blown itself out and it was full light outside. He had been awake for hours in the night trying to warm her, and the hellacious day and late night had combined to make him sleep much later than usual. As he slowly came awake, it took him a minute or two to understand why he felt so incredibly happy and comfortable this morning. When Giselle moved in the circle of his arms, he understood his peaceful, happy mood.

Now this was the way to start out the day! He put a hand flat across her belly and pulled her tighter against him and breathed in the sweet smell of her. She wrapped a leg around his and mumbled something dreamily in Dutch.

She went straight back to sleep again, and in fact, he wondered if she had even really been awake when she had said it. He hoped she still felt that mellow when she realized that he had undressed her and spent the night trying to warm her with his own body heat. He yawned and stretched and decided he'd done what had to be done; he'd done his best to help her and he was so incredibly comfortable right then that he wasn't even going to waste this morning worrying.

He wasn't sure how long he'd lain there enjoying her before she woke up, but finally he knew that she was awake. Her back was to him, so it was impossible to tell what she was thinking and he'd almost begun to worry about her reaction when she stretched lazily and turned in his arms towards him. Her pretty blue eyes looked up at him and she smiled shyly. "Good morning, Trace." She snuggled over tight to him, and though he could no longer see her eyes, he knew that he didn't need to be worrying anymore when she asked, "Do we have to get up today? Or can we just stay like this forever?"

He chuckled as he put a hand up to finger her hair. "I don't know about forever, but I think we'll be fine for a while. How are you feeling this morning?"

She stretched again and sighed. "Very tired and a little achy and stiff." She rested a hand on the muscle of his chest. "And happy." She paused and then said, "You saved me again, didn't you? What happened?"

He shook his head. "I don't even know for sure. I found you sitting next to the wagon with ice on your head, sound asleep. I thought you had come in to change, but when I got in here, I couldn't find you." He hesitated again. "Please forgive me for undressing you, but I had to. I was afraid that you were going to freeze to death."

She leaned her head into him and said, "I don't remember what happened either except that I thought you were trying to kill me for a while last night. My hands hurt so badly. I'm sorry that I got so upset at you."

"It's all okay. I'm sorry that I was hurting you and kept waking you up. I had to, but I'm still sorry. How are your hands this morning?"

She slid them out from under the quilts and turned them back and forth for him. "They're dry. And stiff, but they're okay thanks to you." She put them back under the covers again and turned onto her side against him. "I'm not usually in need of so much rescuing as I have been on this trip. I used to pride myself on doing at least my share, but this is about the fortieth time that you've saved me. Thank you. I'll never be able to get out of your debt I'm afraid."

He let out a deep breath and pulled her closer again. "We've both done our fair share, Giselle. You've more than pulled your weight. In fact, I wish that you hadn't been so concerned with that. It may have cost you your sweet little babies." He put a hand on her belly again. "That's too high a price for doing your portion. I've saved you, but all the way across you've made this trip easier and more organized by what you've done. We'd have never gotten so far, so quickly, without you."

She looked up at him. "Are we going to make it, Trace? Before the snow?"

"We're going to make it, Elle. Before the snow remains to be seen, but we're only days from your valley. We'll make it even if we have to walk in on snowshoes."

"But what about you making it over the California mountains?"

He shrugged. "We'll do our best. That's all we can do. Mose and I may have to wait out the winter somewhere.

We'll just have to see." He didn't tell her that he hoped they got stranded in her valley for the winter. Actually admitting out loud that they were only days from leaving each other made his heart shrivel up. Especially holding her like he was this morning. Walking away from her was going to kill him. He didn't even want to think about it and tried to change back to happier thoughts. It was crazy to waste this only time that he'd get to have her by him this way.

She must have been thinking too, because she was quiet as well and they just lay together, snuggled up in the peace and warmth of the quiet morning. Holding her like this was the ultimate in sweet, but it was also the ultimate in taking all of his self control. Lately, when they'd lain by each other in the night, when he struggled with wanting more from her, he'd begun to pray for strength when it got difficult. Even as nice as her body was, he automatically began to ask for that extra help to take his mind off the fact that she was so pretty and soft and desirable. He tried to just enjoy her without being frustrated, but it took him a while.

Finally, he relaxed and could bask in her again and was doing just that when he heard Dog begin to growl. He groaned right out loud and wanted to swear. He did *not* want to move right now because of some stupid, love-sick Indian brave. "That cussed Indian." He groaned again and leaned up on an elbow. "Sometimes I almost wish that you weren't the world's most exquisite woman, Elle. Is he ever going to give up on you?"

She looked up at him with big eyes when he said that and he laughed at her. "I'm just kidding, Giselle. I'd never want you to be plain, but Jehoshaphat, he's persistent!" He touched her face gently and leaned down and kissed her once, long and slow. "It was awful wondering if you were freezing to death, but this has been about the nicest morning of my life. Thanks."

With that, he pulled back the covers and slipped out and reluctantly began to pull his long underwear back on, grumbling as he did so. "Stupid Indian. I've told him seven thousand times that I'm never going to let you go. You'd think he'd get the message, thick-headed imbecile. It's not like I've ever been hesitant when I've turned him down. Sometimes I wonder if he'll still be dogging us when you're old and gray."

He looked over at her where she was watching him dress, still with those wide, blue eyes. He had the long handles up to his waist and reached for his stockings and boots. Pulling the boots on without lacing them up, he reached over and cupped her cheek. "Sorry, Elle. I guess I can't really blame him. You are pretty desirable. I'm sure he's never seen anyone like you before. I know I haven't."

He stood up and put both hands on the edge of the wagon box and vaulted out. She sat up to watch him through the end of the wagon cover as he strode away towards where Many Feathers sat on his horse. He immediately tore into the Indian in a disgusted tone of voice doing up his buttons. Trace was going on and gesturing both back at the wagon and at his clothes, as he did this Giselle was surprised to see Many Feathers actually blush under his dusky skin.

At that, she blushed herself. She lay back down, wondering what exactly Trace had just told the man in his tirade. She didn't understand the language, but she was pretty sure that Trace had just sworn at the brave in his own tongue. At least that was the distinct impression that she got from his tone of voice. She smiled at Trace as she thought back on the last little while since she had awakened next to him. She blushed again as she thought about how good it had felt to have him so close. He was right-this was about the nicest morning of her life, too. It would be heaven to be able to wake up next to him forever like that.

Sighing, she mentally shook herself. She shouldn't let her thoughts go there. He had just reminded her that they had only days left until she would probably never see him again. Pausing before she got up to dress, she wondered how in the world she was ever going to face being the second wife of an older man when she got to the valley after being with Trace like this. She sat up and tucked the blankets under her arms. It was going to be awful. Remembering the muscles of his chest under her hands this morning, she shook her head. She didn't think she could even do it.

The brethren were probably going to be completely disgusted with her, but she honestly didn't think that marrying another man was an option after the way she had grown to love Trace. And after some of the things that he'd said just now, she was a little mixed up. He almost acted like he really loved her, and even said things from time to time that sounded like forever. But she knew that he still had every intention of trying to reach California after dropping her in the valley-which was probably for the best anyway, because he wasn't a member of the church.

With a grimace, she looked out at him striding back toward the wagon. Trying to figure out how to deal with both her feelings and reality was going to be the hardest thing she'd ever done. Trace leaned his head back into the wagon and looked at her sitting there, still in the blankets. He studied her face before he quietly asked, "What's wrong?"

She didn't understand what he was asking. "What do you mean?"

"You don't look very happy all of a sudden. Is something wrong?"

Thinking about that for a minute, she wondered how to answer that. Everything was wrong. How could they have such a nice morning and then just plan to walk away from each other? But then that had been the plan all along, so maybe nothing was wrong at all, but she was incredibly sad about it anyway. But what to tell him?

Theirs had been such a sweet and simple friendship and she had always felt comfortable talking to him, but she felt a little foolish telling him that she wanted to stay with him when he went on to California. Finally, she just decided to be matter-of-fact about it all. She shook her head and admitted, "Nothing's wrong, Trace. I'm just going to have a terribly hard time telling you goodbye in a few days."

She changed the subject. "What did you say to Many Feathers?" The brave had lost no time in heading straight out after Trace's tongue lashing. She smiled. "I don't speak Indian, but that sounded suspiciously like swearing from here."

Trace chuckled and climbed back into the wagon, slipped off his boots, began to pull his pants on, and put on his shirt and coat. "I'm not admitting anything to you, girl. He got my point, I'm sure. It probably won't dissuade him from wanting you, but at least he knows that I'm not considering his offers by any means."

He put on his hat, dug in the pocket of his coat, and donned leather gloves. "I'm sorry. I may have ruined your dress last night. At any rate, it will probably never be the same after that storm. It's still soaked and sitting on the floor up by the seat with your petticoats. Be sure and dress warmly. Pneumonia wouldn't be out of the question after what you went through last night. Sit tight here and I'll bring you some breakfast."

He went to climb back out and she put a hand on his arm to stop him. "No, Trace. I'll get up and get the breakfast and bring it to you. You do whatever else needs doing. I'm fine."

"Giselle, everything out here is covered with ice and completely waterlogged. It's going to be a trick just to get a fire going. Stay down and rest while I see to it."

She reached into a satchel to find underclothing. "No, Trace. We're in this together. I tire easily sometimes, but I'm fine and we need to hurry. I'll rest when we're on the trail." She tried to make him understand. "I want to be honorable, Trace. I need to be part of this trip, not just a burden. I'll be careful, I promise. If I don't feel good, I'll tell you."

She slipped a chemise over her head and began to lace it up. He looked at her steadily for a minute and then nodded. In a gentle voice he said, "All right, Elle. But you promised. And you have to rest when we get going. Agreed?"

"Agreed. Do you, by any chance, know where my boots ended up?" She started rooting around under the quilts and then looked up when she caught him watching her with quiet eyes. "What?"

He shook his head. "Nothing." He reached into the corner of the wagon and drew out her boots and began to feel inside them to see how wet they were. "They're still a little damp. Do you have any others you can wear?" She met his eyes and nodded without answering. "Good. Let these dry for the day here in the wagon." He was still watching her with unfathomable eyes as he hopped out of the wagon again. "I'll get the cow milked."

When she made it out of the wagon fully dressed and started to pull wood out from under the wagon sling, he was surprised. "I wish I'd known that wood was there last night. I didn't realize that you'd put any down there. I didn't even try to start a fire in that wet. I might have been able to get you warm faster."

She looked up at him and then said, "Then I'm glad that you didn't know it was there." She turned and went to finish starting the fire while he just stared at her for a second.

Trace thought about what she had just said and then he turned and went to do his own chores as well, but he couldn't get that comment out of his head. What had she meant? The whole time he milked and fed, hitched up and rearranged the wagon, he tried to figure out what she had inferred by that comment, but the only thing that he could come up with was that she was glad that he had ended up skin to skin with her instead of using a fire.

He was so confused about it that he finally just asked her outright when he helped her back into the wagon box. She gave him a shy smile and then was frank in her sweet, Dutch accent. "Waking up next to you was much nicer than the fire, Trace. I must be honest." She looked at him with those bright eyes and he was more confused than ever. She was pretty up front with him. Why was he having such a hard time figuring out what she was thinking?

CHAPTER 12

The weather was remarkably clear considering how nasty the storm had been. The ice melted off and even the sucking mud began to dry up by early afternoon. They left the river valley and entered a wide plain of low, rolling, sagebrush covered hills that stretched to the western horizon. He was glad that the weather had calmed because there was nothing to break that bleak wind out here if it picked up. He drove the hours away, thinking.

There were a number of things on his mind and the day seemed to fly. He had all but given up on catching the other wagons. Their tracks were still days old and they would be clear into the valley long before he and Giselle could make up the distance. He thought about her and how he felt about her for hours, and when he couldn't figure out what to do with those feelings and their situation, he tried to put her out of his mind and ended up thinking about the journal he had been reading those days ago.

Josiah and Petja's thoughts and beliefs had been enlightening, the more he learned of Giselle and her character and honesty, the more the Mormon beliefs intrigued him. She was smart and sharp as well as being kind, hardworking, and honorable. He had to wonder what would so touch her about her religion that she would give up what she had and put up with what she had to pursue it. When she leaned over the wagon box after lunch and hesitantly asked if she could get up now, he was grateful for her company. There were a thousand things that he wanted to ask her.

All the rest of that afternoon and into the evening as he drove he asked her questions and she answered him. He wanted to know both about her religion's beliefs and what she and the other Saints had been through to get to where they were. By the time that he stopped the wagon when it was too dark to see where they were going any longer, he knew much more about the Mormons and had even more questions than when they'd begun talking.

There was no shelter of any kind and they made dry camp with only the wood that was still in the sling and sticks from the sage brush bushes. The sage smelled terrible as it burned and their dinner tasted a little like it, but they were hungry enough that they didn't even care.

Trace had wondered that day if going to bed that night would be uncomfortable after their interesting night the night before, but he should have known that they'd be fine. They were good enough friends and were tired enough that bedding down was completely normal. They prayed and snuggled up to each other and as they drifted off, he asked her what a *flanel bord geschiedenis* was.

She sleepily tried to explain the idea of a story stuck to a board covered with flannel and he laughed. No wonder she'd been more comfortable. He held her gently, wishing that he didn't feel like such a flannel board story in his long handles himself. Last night had been an eye opener for him that way as well. He would never look at long underwear the same again.

Waking in the dark the next morning was reality compared to the heavenly morning before, but the feel of another storm in the air had them both up and moving immediately anyway. The clouds had kept the frigid, cold temperatures at bay, but the damp, biting wind more than made up for it with its icy chill. They raced through chores and breakfast and Trace began hitching up in record time. Giselle finished packing the last of the camp gear and was gathering the eggs and feeding the chickens when she heard Trace begin to cuss the rogue mule. It always seemed to pick the days with questionable weather to act up.

She came around from the back of the wagon with five eggs in her skirt just as the mule began to raise a ruckus as Trace went to finish hitching up. As he leaned to hook the trace on the single tree, the mule reared and rammed into the harness. The free end of the single tree swung and the iron hook on the end of it slammed Trace in the side of the head before he could jump out of the way.

He went down like a rock. Giselle dropped her eggs and ran to try to calm the mule before Trace was trampled to death or run over by the dragging wagon. After several minutes, when the mule had settled down enough that she dared leave its side, she went to him and was horrified to find him still out cold, lying literally between the mule's hind feet and the front wheel of the wagon.

Praying like never before, she took hold of his leg and tried to pull him out of the way. She couldn't believe how heavy he was as she struggled for all she was worth to budge him even a few inches. It took her almost ten minutes and several prayers to find the strength to move him enough that she wasn't terrified that the mule would kill him with its fool antics.

With him moved, Giselle hooked up the offending trace and then wondered what in the world to do next. She went to Trace and began talking to him and patting his face. She even brought water from the bucket to splash on his face in hopes of making him come to. He didn't even flinch and she stared at the first huge, fat flakes of snow that began to fall sideways from the force of the cold wind all around them.

The snow falling on his face didn't faze him, but it made her feel an incredible fear in her heart. She had hardly even been able to move him. How was she ever going to get him into the wagon and head on towards the valley without his help? For the first time, she was facing this journey without his stalwart strength beside her and it scared her. It scared her a lot.

Trying to push back the fear, she dropped to her knees there beside him and told the Father about her troubles and fears, how she needed to hurry to get across this wide expanse of rolling sage hills to find shelter so that they didn't all freeze to death in this exposure. She begged for his help and then sat with her head bowed as she finished to listen and absorb the sweet peace that her prayer had brought her.

It was as if her Father in Heaven was gently telling her that she needed to pull herself together and have faith that she could handle whatever she needed to with His help and her work. After sitting for a minute, she studied the situation in front of her and tried to think things through. The first thing she needed to do was find a way to get Trace into the wagon and then find someplace to get out of the weather and wind as soon as she could.

The only idea that she could come up with to get him into the wagon was to hook ropes to the hoops that held the wagon cover and somehow lift him in. If she used her grandfather's pulleys from his tool box, and ropes in a couple of places so that she didn't have to try to lift all of his weight at once, she hoped she would be able to do it. She set to work, unlaced the wagon cover at the back of the wagon, rigged up the ropes and pulleys.

She had to try maneuver the wagon to where she could get him lifted up without accidentally running over him or getting him stepped on. He was lying there in the falling snow without even a slicker, and she got a canvas tarp and covered him with it until she was ready to lift him. She got out his slicker and put it on herself and then rolled up the sleeves several inches to try to make it less cumbersome to work in.

As the storm grew in intensity, she prayed again and picked up the mule's lines and began the delicate process of moving the wagon around to where she could lift him into the back. Praying all the while, it seemed to take forever to maneuver it to where she thought she could lift him. She set the brake, tied off the lines and jumped down.

Her hands were already freezing as she began to rig up the ropes to him, wishing that she had a pair of leather gloves like he had to work in in this wind driven snow. She kept reminding herself of the reassurance that her prayer had brought as she struggled to untangle her ropes and pulleys and get ready to lift Trace. She hooked one rope over his thighs and one around his shoulders and finally began to pull with all of her might. She was discouraged to tears when she could lift him only a few inches with one rope, and she found that she couldn't tie it off to go pull on the other without it slipping and letting him fall back to the ground. She tried time after time to no avail, and at length, dropped to her knees to pray one more time for inspiration.

Upon saying amen, she resolutely wiped at her tears and climbed back up into the wagon to dig through her grandfather's tool box in hopes of finding a magical fix to her dilemma. She was so busy digging that at first she didn't hear Dog growl until he started to snarl in earnest. She dropped the lid of the tool box and was just about to scramble to the flaps of the wagon cover when they were brushed abruptly aside. Dog was still raising a commotion and suddenly Many Feathers' head appeared inside the flaps.

She gasped in panic, but then she realized that he was holding Trace. As she met his eyes, he unceremoniously lifted him and dumped him roughly over the side of the wagon box into the bed below and ducked back out of the flaps. Hurriedly, she went to Trace and wiped the snow and water off of him as best she could and pulled their bedding up and over him snuggly. Then she went to climb out of the wagon herself.

As she reached the opening, she met Many Feathers again. He handed her the coiled ropes and pulleys without expression and bent to fold and roll the tarp and handed her that as well. Without a word, he turned and walked to his horse and mounted and then turned towards her as if he was waiting.

Wondering what he was up to, she secured the wagon cover back over the hoops and tied the flaps closed, hurriedly tethered the cow and calf in place, and then clamored onto the seat. After brushing the snow off, she untied the lines and snapped them at the mules, and glancing around one last time, headed up the trail behind Many Feathers' snow-whitened horse.

Giselle had no idea what he was up to, but she would be eternally grateful for his help in lifting Trace into the wagon. She honestly didn't know how she would have ever gotten him in without his help. She prayed again in gratitude and wondered if Many Feathers realized that he had been the answer to prayer just now. She looked ahead to his silhouette that was blurred by the thickening storm and wished that she could speak his language to thank him.

She drove the wagon up the trail that became less and less discernable in the deepening snow and searched all around them for any sign of a place where they could turn off to find shelter. There were occasional hills and even some cliffs around the creek bed, but there wasn't much that looked promising in the short distance before the snow cut off visibility.

At one point, there was a steep bank off to the left, and she started to pull the wagon into its meager shelter when Many Feathers turned back and spoke to her. He was shaking his head and gesturing to the fore and she hesitated, wondering what to do. Finally, she looked at him and he met her eyes and said something with conviction and pointed. She nodded and slapped the reins to the mules and headed on. He wanted her to follow him and she decided that she would do just that. He didn't seem to be trying to harm her and she felt like she should trust him just now.

By the time Many Feathers reached their destination, the snow was eight or ten inches deep and the mules were having a hard pull of it. When Giselle realized that he had led her directly to a large cave in the bend of the creek bank, she was indescribably grateful. She pulled the wagon up alongside the opening to the cave and hadn't even gotten the brake set and the lines tied off before Many Feathers spoke to her, nodded, and rode off into the gathering gloom of the storm. She wished there was a way to thank him, but she didn't even have the chance before he disappeared.

She climbed down from the wagon seat and on looking around for a minute, untied the cow and calf and led them into a cleft in the bank that was sheltered on three sides and tied them. She went back and was unhitching the mules when Many Feathers appeared again with a whole huge, dead cedar tree that he dragged into the opening of the cave. He turned around and reached into the back of the wagon and picked Trace up, blankets and all, and carried him into the cave. Then he dumped him onto the ground with the same degree of roughness that he had piled him into the wagon with. At that, he turned back to Giselle, gave her a deep, solemn look, and once again mounted his horse and headed back out into the snow.

Giselle finished tying the mules, gave them a bait of corn and then began to set up camp, wondering if Many Feathers was going to suddenly reappear again out of the blizzard. She explored the cave and found that it was actually a series of three caves, one after the other, that extended back into the fold of the hill above the stream.

The cave in the front was large and open with a sandy floor. It necked down into a smaller room that was still roughly ten or eleven feet across and then opened into an even smaller room that was only about nine feet deep and five feet high. The second room had the remnants of many fires in one corner and Giselle looked up to see how someone had had fires in here without smoking themselves out. In the blackened ceiling, pale light shone through and she could see a crack that had allowed the smoke to escape up and out.

Once again, she was incredibly grateful for Many Feathers' help. The caves were far and away more than she could ever have asked for just now. She glanced over at Trace's unconscious form and knelt one more time to whisper a prayer of thanks. A few hours ago, she had thought that she wasn't up to much alone, but now, with the cave and firewood, she was going to be okay. It was her turn to rescue Trace for once.

She struggled and pulled Trace into the second room and stretched him out as much as possible. He was still completely out and had a huge goose egg on his head where the iron had struck him. She refused to even allow herself to worry that he wouldn't be okay eventually and set about making a fire and setting up camp. It was only early afternoon, but she knew that they were going nowhere until this storm broke. Even in the lee of the creek bank, she was already standing in more than a foot of snow to load gear out of the wagon.

She brought the rest of the bedding, made a bed and rolled Trace into it and then began to make dinner over the fire in the corner. The second cave was almost luxuriously dry, and when she hung a blanket over the opening to keep the wind out it was relatively cozy, all things considered. She hoped that Many Feathers had found someplace this warm and dry to wait the storm out. She was grateful to him, but she was also a little afraid of him still. She brought her grandfather's pistol in and then had Dog lie at the opening of the main cave, just in case. She didn't necessarily want to shoot Many Feathers, but if he was somewhere around, she wanted to know it first when Trace was so out of it.

She cooked, ate, and cleaned up, and after checking on Trace again, went back to the wagon and brought the wash kettle in and filled it. As long as they were stuck here, she was going to take advantage of it. She did the wash, strung a line, and hung the clothes to dry. She made bread and even brought the copper bath tub in and had a luxuriously warm bath there in the firelight with the storm raging outside. Trace still hadn't moved a muscle and she was beginning to struggle not to worry. She went and got her Book of Mormon and a candle and climbed into the bed with him and tried to read to get her mind off of things.

The storm grew in intensity until it seemed to scream past the cave opening. She got up and brought the stock and the chickens right into the first cave and then went back to lie next to Trace one more time. By the time it was full dark, she had decided that even the wolves would have taken shelter somewhere in this gale. She banked the fire, blew out her candle, and went to bed.

Even out cold, Trace was still somehow reassuring to lie next to and she prayed that he would be okay and that they'd still make it to the valley safely. Then, trusting to Dog to keep watch, she snuggled close to Trace and went to sleep.

The only way she knew it was morning the next day was that there was a lighter strip of sky showing through the crack in the roof of the cave. The fire had long since burned down and, with the blanket over the opening, there was no other light to speak of. Outside of the covers it was cool and she decided to snuggle against Trace's warmth for a minute before she got up to light the fire again. He moved in his sleep and gave a low groan, but when she talked to him, all he did was pull her tight into his arms and sigh.

His strength, even in his sleep, nearly crushed her, but it was reassuring nonetheless. She pulled at his hands to get him to loosen up and then turned towards his chest and cuddled up to his body heat. She had had no idea that sleeping beside a husband would be this nice. It was incredible.

She spoke to him, but he was more than just asleep still and only moved a little at her words. He had one iron arm around her waist and she gave up the idea of getting up just then and happily closed her eyes again to lie there. His chest against her cheek was deliciously comforting as she went back to sleep.

It must have been an hour or more later that Trace tightened his hold and woke her up. She could hardly breathe and she tried to rouse him again. He still didn't hear her talking to him and she took hold of his hands to try to loosen them. It almost felt like he was resisting her on purpose and he rolled over towards her. Then it was not only hard to breathe, but she could hardly move.

"Trace." She sighed and pushed against him. "Tracey. You're squishing me!" She patted his face with both hands and he leaned into her neck and breathed against her throat. "Trace!" She started into him, talking fast, trying to get him to wake up and help her.

Finally, she felt him kiss her neck softly and say, "English, Elle. English." He finally rolled off slowly. "Giselle." He moaned and put a hand to his head. "I'm sorry, sweetheart, but I don't understand Dutch."

She took a deep breath of air as he loosened his hold and rolled over. "Trace." She leaned up to look at him. "Oh, Trace, I've been so worried. Are you okay?"

He grimaced and looked at her through narrowed eyes. "I'm not sure." He looked all around. "Where are we?" He put the hand back to his head. "And why do I feel like I've been kicked in the head by a mule?"

She bent to kiss the goose egg that was slowly going down. "Close enough. The mule tried to kill you, but it wasn't a kick, it was the single tree that hit you. Yesterday morning, when we were trying to leave. Do you remember?"

He started to shake his head and then groaned again. "I don't remember a thing. We were out in the sage. How did we get here?" He looked around again at the cave walls.

At first she started to explain everything, but she could see that he wasn't very with it and just said, "I drove here. There's been a terrible storm. Many Feathers helped me find these caves." She started to push him away to get up and start the fire, but he took one of her hands and held it.

"Don't get up. Stay with me for a second." She lay back down next to him and he said, "What were you saying just now? In Dutch? You didn't sound very happy."

She shook her head against him. "I wasn't unhappy. I just couldn't breathe. You were holding me so tight and then rolled on me."

Slowly he lifted his arm and put it over her. "Sorry. I didn't even realize."

"It's okay, but you're hard to move when you're out of it. I had no idea you were so big. I couldn't even move to get out from under your shoulder."

His breath was still against her neck when he said, "I've always been big. Mose was the only boy my age that was bigger than me." He paused for a minute and then said absently, "I'm hungry." With hardly a pause, he continued, "I think that I should learn to speak Dutch. Then I could understand what you say when you're upset. You switch over and then go talking about lickety split and I never have a bit of an idea what you're trying to tell me. I wish I knew Dutch." He kissed her gently on the neck again.

Wondering what in the world was going on with him, she sat up and looked at him. He rolled over to look at her blankly. "Do you have to leave, Elle? I was comfortable with you here."

His kissing flustered her completely and she decided that she'd better get up now. She was relatively sure that he had no idea what he was even doing and she really wanted to kiss him back. When he was more with it, he'd probably be embarrassed if she did.

She pulled back the covers, jumped up, wrapped a shawl around herself, and went over and rekindled the fire. When the fire was good and going, she put several more pieces of wood on it and hopped back under the covers again with Trace. He'd been watching her at the fire, and when she got back in, he said, "Put your feet over on me and get them warm." He took both of her hands in his and rubbed them until they were warm. Then he pulled her tight against his chest with a little, happy sigh. "It's nice to have you by me here, Elle."

This mellow, easy-going cuddliness almost made her a little wary. She loved it, but she wasn't sure that he was very aware of what he was doing. That had been a pretty severe whack on the head. For a few more minutes, while the fire started to take hold of the wood, she worried. Then she decided that worrying wasn't going to help anything and just enjoyed being cuddled while he was a bit looped. It wouldn't hurt anything, and it was what she really wanted anyway. With that thought, she turned her back to him and leaned back into him so they were like spoons, and made a happy sound of her own.

CHAPTER 13

It wasn't very long before Trace went back to sleep again, just long enough for him to stroke her shoulder and kiss her neck again several times. Just when she had decided that she had to turn around to him and kiss him back, she felt him relax against her and begin to snore. She let out a big breath of frustration, pulled back the blankets, and slipped out of bed.

The air in the second cave was still cool and Giselle dressed for the day warmly. Maybe being fully clothed would ward off some of the physical attraction that was thick in the cave this morning. When she was dressed, she sat down on the bed next to him to put on her stockings and boots, and found that she was still tempted to climb back in and wake him up.

Getting up with a sigh, she decided that having the bed as the only place to sit was probably more than foolish. Stranded here as they were, she decided that, just as soon as she had the stock cared for and breakfast ready, she would go out and wrestle her grandmother's rocking chair out of the wagon and bring it inside to sit on.

When she finally got out there to move the rocking chair in, she found that "wrestle" had been the operative word for sure. She hadn't remembered the rocker being that hard to move when they'd loaded it last July. After struggling with it for more than half an hour, when she finally got it moved to the back of the wagon where their bed had been, she was breathing heavily. Just then, Trace poked his head through the wagon flaps. He looked at her, sitting there in the rocker, with her faced flushed from exertion, and asked, "What are you doing out here, Giselle? Are you okay?"

Feeling a little foolish, she answered, "I'm just trying to get this rocker inside the cave to have something to sit on, but it's grown a great deal since I helped load it in here. It's been difficult to move and I had to stop and rest for a moment."

"Here, let me lift it for you." She could almost have cussed him when he lifted it effortlessly. She followed him back into the cave and then back out to the wagon when he turned and went back out. He lifted their wooden, lidded grub box and brought it in as well. "It looks like we're going to be here for a bit until the storm breaks. Might as well make it easier to cook and get things done." He looked up at the low, ragged, gray sky. "How long have we been here? Have I been out for days, or has it snowed this much fast?"

She gave the lowering storm ceiling a worried glance. "It started yesterday morning. We've been here since early yesterday afternoon, but there was nearly a foot by the time we got here. It's just coming down heavy and fast."

He seemed to mimic her worried look as he said, "I don't think your wagon load is going to make it to your valley this fall, Elle. I'm sorry, but unless it stops snowing right now and gets warm in a hurry, this wagon is going to be stuck here awhile." After setting the grub box near the fire in the corner, he went back into the next cave to look around. "How did you ever find this place? This is great!"

Recounting what had happened after Trace was knocked cold, she ended with voicing her wish that she could have thanked Many Feathers and hoped that he was somewhere warm and dry as well. Trace laughed. "That Indian is probably somewhere right close by, buttoned up as snug as we are, Elle. I doubt that you need to worry about him. Where there's one cave, there are probably several."

"Oh, good. He was so good to help me. I'll quit worrying about him and just worry about finding feed for the mules and cows now. And about how we're going to get through this much snow to get to the valley."

Trace put an arm around her shoulders. "Worrying isn't going to help anything, Giselle. Let's just do what we can and let the rest go. We'll pack your stuff in here and wall off that back cave. Maybe, if we leave a medicine man's talisman, it will still be here in the spring and we'll come get it. Follow me and I'll show you something. The animals are going to be fine. They'll do the same thing the elk and deer do when the snow gets too deep to graze."

He took her to the front cave and she watched as indeed, the mules leaned their heads over the rope she had used as a corral and were nipping at the willows and bushes that grew nearby. "They'll browse off the tender branches of the bushes just like an elk would. We'll be fine. It'll be a trip that you'll always remember, but we'll be fine."

They went back into the second cave. He sat down on the grub box and stretched his hands to the fire. Rubbing the goose egg on the side of his head, he asked, "The single tree did this?"

She nodded as she dished him up some of the breakfast she had left warming. "That sweet-natured mule lunged just as you went to hook up the trace. You landed almost under its back feet, right in front of the wagon wheel. I was terrified that you would be killed. Then I couldn't move you. You weigh several thousand pounds, I'm afraid. I finally got you away from the mule and the wheels, but I couldn't lift you into the wagon for anything, even with my grandfather's pulleys and ropes. If Many Feathers hadn't come and lifted you, we'd still be sitting there in the sage, with you buried in the snow by now. His showing up was an answer to my prayers."

Trace stretched and groaned. "My head hurts, but so does the rest of me. I feel like I was run over by the wagon."

Giselle smiled up at him sweetly. "That would be because Many Feathers threw you into and out of the wagon like a sack of flour. He helped me, but it was none too gentle. If I hadn't been so incredibly grateful for him lifting you at all, I would have been outraged. He pretty well just dumped you in and then dumped you back out onto the floor there." She pointed.

Groaning again, Trace laughed. "I am his competition after all." He finished his breakfast and then climbed back into the bed to stretch out. Within minutes he was out again and she was back to square one of trying to get her mind on other things than him lying there. She dug out the knitting that she had been struggling with this whole trip. If they were going to walk or ride the mules out, heavy stockings were in order.

She tried to untangle the needles and yarn and couldn't help smiling to herself as she did it. There was no doubt that any stockings that she succeeded in knitting would make for interesting wearing, that was for sure. It was a good thing that warmth didn't depend on how something looked or she would be in trouble.

She had been up and cooking for a while when Trace lifted his head again. The goose egg was down, but that look in his eyes when he looked at her was still there, and Giselle was sure that bringing the rocker in had been a good idea. When he got up, he surprised her by going out and bringing in Petja's table and chairs as well. He set them up on the other side of the fire and said, "We might as well use them while we're here since they need to be brought in and stored anyway."

That was the first time they had ever sat across the table from each other to eat, and it was a surprisingly nice dinner there in the cave together. It was nice enough that she almost wished they could just stay there indefinitely and not have to face hiking out and telling each other goodbye.

That goodbye was on her mind again when she lay down next to him that night at bedtime. She was torn between enjoying his closeness and warmth and worrying that she should keep her distance and try to protect her heart from being crushed when the time came. Deciding that Trace had been right, that worrying wouldn't help and that she was already going to be crushed, she snuggled over against him in spite of herself. When he turned and gathered her close, there was no hope of staying away anyway.

He was still slightly out of it and she woke up late in the night, nearly strangled in his arms. When she tried to loosen his grip, he sighed and leaned his head to begin kissing her neck again. This time, she was far too tempted and got clear up and stoked the fire. What was she going to do about him? She ended up wrapping a quilt around herself and attempting to knit by the firelight. Knitting helped. She was terrible at it even when there was good light. Between trying to concentrate on what she was doing, and trying not to laugh at the mess she was creating, she was somewhat able to forget about Trace's kisses.

He woke her there in the rocker the next morning. He was rubbing her neck and shoulders. "What are you doing up in the chair, Elley? Were you having trouble sleeping?" She nodded sleepily and he asked, "Are you worrying about the snow?"

He was watching her and she wondered what to tell him. "No. Not the snow, exactly."

He leaned down next to her chair. "What then exactly?" His voice was gentle and she worried that he could read her mind and she dropped her eyes.

"Oh, just things, you know."

"No, I don't know. I'm not sure that I like having a chair in here after all. You've never left me in bed to go worry by yourself before. Are we not good enough friends that you can tell me what's wrong?"

She looked up, hesitating, and then leveled with him. "You're just very affectionate when you have a head injury. I'm not entirely sure how to take you is all. I'm sure when you feel better you'll be back to normal."

Still meeting her eyes steadily, he asked, "What did I do?"

She shrugged and dropped her eyes once more. "It's nothing really. You're just more snuggly than normal. It makes me worry about how I'm going to tell you goodbye."

"What did I do, Elle?" She went to shrug again and he asked more earnestly, "Did I offend you?"

"No!" She hurried to reassure him. "No, Trace. You just kiss me in your sleep sometimes and it makes me want to kiss you back. When you're back to normal, it would embarrass you, I'm sure, so I just had to get up so that I didn't... So that... I just had to get up is all. We're friends, I promise. I just worry. Telling you goodbye is going to be hard as it is." He stayed there beside her chair, searching her face for a few seconds and then stood up.

He squeezed her shoulder. "I'm sorry that I make you worry, Elle. Please forgive me. I'll try to do better."

She shook her head. "I don't think the problem lies with you, Trace. It's just me. We're fine, I promise."

He leaned back down and cupped her cheek with his hand. "I know we're fine, Elle. We always have been. We always will be. But don't feel like you have to get up to get away from me. Just elbow me or something, and I'll straighten up."

It wasn't exactly that easy, but she wasn't going to tell him that. She smiled. "Okay, Trace. I'll elbow you. What would you like to eat this morning?" She began to roll her yarn around her work and the needles.

He took it from her and unrolled it, and with a twinkle in his eye, asked her, "What exactly is it that you're making?"

Knowing that the glob of light pink yarn was completely unrecognizable, she sweetly smiled and replied, "Some lovely, warm stockings for you, Trace. I want you to be nice and warm for our trek out. You're going to love them!" He laughed and rolled the whole mess up again.

"I'm sure that I will. Are they going to be finished in time?"

Still smiling sweetly, she assured him, "Absolutely. I will work very hard to have them done for you. Wait and see." He chuckled and shook his head as he built up the fire.

Theirs had been a good theory, but bringing herself to elbow Trace that night in his sleep was next to impossible. Giselle had actually started to kiss him back before she caught herself and quickly got up and escaped to her rocker again. She was careful to be up and working by the time that Trace awoke so that she didn't have to face him about running away again, but she knew that he knew that something was up by the way he watched her warily that morning. She was almost shy around him today and didn't want to have to admit why. By mid-afternoon she was decidedly tired, and when he sat at the table with Josiah's journal, she climbed back into their bed with a sigh for a nap.

He was still at the table, completely engrossed in the book when she woke up and she was surprised that he would be so interested in a book that was written in Dutch. When he realized that she was awake, he started to ask her questions again about the Church, and all that had transpired between their first meeting with the missionaries on a trip to England, and the time they ended up in St. Joseph, Missouri, ready to start across with the wagon train. For nearly two hours they sat like that, talking, until she finally got up and went outside to milk the cow. The bushes near the mouth of the cave were stripped to nothing, so she came back in and got a knife and went back out into the storm to cut branches and bushes for the stock to chew on. Trace appeared a minute or two later to help her, and in short order, they had the stock fed and bedded down again.

Back inside, they worked side by side to make dinner and then sat at Petja's table to eat it. Trace brought the little book right to the table and began to ask her questions about it. She finally asked him, "I thought you said that you didn't understand Dutch. How can you read it when you don't understand it?"

He looked at her like he thought that she'd gone crazy. "I can't read Dutch, Giselle. What are you talking about?"

Picking up the book, she began on the page that he had open and read it aloud. It was written in Dutch. He looked shocked and snatched it from her hand and stared at it for a second. Then he looked at her in complete confusion. He paged back a few pages and then turned back to the first and looked up, still confused. He didn't say a word, just looked at her, and then shook his head. "Giselle, I've been reading this book for weeks, from the very first day that you collapsed on the wagon. I've been able to read it just fine. I've never even noticed that it wasn't written in English."

At first she thought he was kidding her, and then when she realized that he was serious, the hair on the back of her neck began to stand on end. "You could read it?" He nodded. "And you understood it all?"

"Every word. Now that you pointed it out, it's completely foreign." She looked at him again, wondering if he was playing a joke, but he wasn't.

Their eyes met for a long moment and she wondered out loud, "Is that some form of the gift of tongues?"

"I don't know what it is, but I know that I've been reading this journal for weeks and it has helped me."

"What do you mean, it has helped you?"

He hesitated. "It has been very thought provoking. I've learned about your grandparents and their wonderful relationship and it's helped me to understand more about your religion and why the Mormons have done the things they have. It's definitely helped me to understand you better."

Wondering what he meant, she looked at him, worried. "What has it helped you to understand better about me? What would there be about me that you wouldn't understand anyway?"

"Oh maybe things like the fact that you are Dutch, or Mormon, or especially that you're female. How's a poor, uneducated lout like me supposed to understand that without a little help from Josiah and Petja?"

"Poor, uneducated lout?" She laughed at him, but then picked up the book to thumb through it. "What's in here that would help you understand females?"

"This book," He took it from her almost reverently, "has a great many pearls of wisdom for a simple boy like me." He paused as he turned pages. "Whether I'll ever be able to read it and understand it again is the question." He glanced up at Giselle. "Will it come back? The gift of tongues? Will I ever be able to read and understand Dutch again?"

She shook her head. "You're asking me, Trace? I thought this little book helped you understand me. If that was the case, you'd know that I can't answer a question like that. You'll have to ask someone far more spiritually in tune than me."

He thought about that for a minute and then gently said, "I've never known anyone more spiritually in tune than you, Elle. In my whole life, I've never been around someone with a spirit about them like you."

She leaned across the table and patted his hand. "That's kind of you to say that, Trace, but I'm sure you're mistaken. Mose is the only friend of yours that I know very well, but he's far more in tune than me."

Trace was quiet for a minute while he considered that. "I wonder if Mose would know if the understanding will come back." He was thoughtful for another second and then asked, "Would you read it to me, Giselle? I'm almost done with it. I only have about a fifth of it left. Would you mind?"

"No, of course not. Do you want me to read it to you tonight?"

"Is there anything else that you need to do right now?"

She smiled, "Just knit your stockings. Here." She got up and handed him the tangled, lumpy yarn. "I'll read, you knit. It will probably look much better that way."

Trace chuckled at her as she came back to sit at the table. "It'll come, Elley. Just be patient. It may never be your gift, but you'll figure it out eventually, just like you've figured out everything else."

CHAPTER 14

That night in bed, Giselle thought about those words. She hadn't figured everything else out. She certainly hadn't figured out how to deal with his physical affection when she was lying beside him. He was being exceptionally snuggly again in his sleep, and she was worrying more than ever about trying to learn to live without him.

She thought about Brother Gibson, the older man that had approached her about becoming his second wife, and nearly groaned just at the thought. There was no way she was going to be able to just go on with her life as if she'd never known and fallen in love with Trace. His breath on her neck gave her goose bumps, and she slipped out of bed to retreat to the rocking chair again. Trace thought they were only a week or two from the valley. She'd just have to get more thick-skinned between now and then.

The next day, Trace seemed more like himself and she hoped that his head was finally healed up from being struck so hard. She read to him for an hour or so in the afternoon and then again in the evening after dinner. It had been interesting, reading her grandparents' thoughts to him, until she got to the place where they recorded what had happened the night she was attacked.

When she realized what was coming, she swallowed hard and tried to make her heart stay calm and her stomach behave, but she had to get up and rush out of the cave to be sick in the snow. She hadn't started to translate what was coming and Trace had no idea what was going on when she stopped so abruptly and all the blood drained from her face. He followed her out and put a hand on her back as she was sick and then handed her a handkerchief as she stood back up, his eyes studying her, trying to understand.

She turned away from him and when they were back in the cave, she quietly closed the book. "Let's don't read anymore tonight, Trace. I'm tired. Can we just go to bed?"

Still watching her, he nodded, "Sure. Whatever is fine, Giselle." She undressed and slid between the quilts, still sick to her stomach, while Trace watched her without saying anything. When she was in and quiet, he banked the fire, and blew out the candle and undressed and climbed in beside her, obviously wondering what was going on, but she couldn't tell him. She couldn't even think about it and willed her mind to think of anything else.

Without realizing it, she turned away from him, pulled herself into as little a ball as she could, and for a good half hour, battled her mind to go anywhere but to thoughts about that awful, black night.

She tried, but it was hopeless. The memories of that night hit her like a sledgehammer. Once more she had to run out into the snow, only now bare footed, with Trace right behind her. This time when she lay back down beside him, he went to pull her into his embrace, but she still couldn't face him and pulled away.

He kept at her until she finally let him pull her against his chest there in the dark, and she couldn't help the tears that came in a rush. She still tried to think of something else, but just reading those few words until she'd understood what was coming had completely overcome her, and she couldn't seem to get her thoughts under control. Her heart began to pound and it was hard to breathe and the tears hit with a wall of fear and revulsion.

She didn't know how long it was before she felt Trace pulling her tighter and tighter against him, and even though he was almost starting to hurt her, it helped. She was able to focus on him and his strength and leave a little bit of the fear and horror of that night behind. Slowly, she began to listen to him speaking her name and hugging her painfully tight, and she mentally rolled into him just as she had those nights on the trail when the wolves had frightened her. He had no way of knowing what was going on, but still he held her and told her over and over that he had her and that she was okay here with him.

Finally, she began to understand that she was indeed safe, that never again would she be treated the way she had then, and that Trace could protect her even mentally from the hateful men that had hurt her so badly both physically and emotionally. She understood then that the terrible memories could be pushed back and that she didn't have to let them overwhelm her tonight here in his arms.

At length, she got a handle on the tears and her racing heart, and she clung to Trace like he was a port in a maelstrom of fearful memories. He still held her tight and she could begin to feel where he stroked her hair and shoulder and back as he continued to talk to her in her ear over and over, telling her that she was okay.

Eventually, the reality of him and his strength overcame the illusions in her head and heart and she let herself be drawn into his touch and she turned away from the fear that her thoughts had brought on. Exactly opposite of the other nights, she tried to focus on him and his hands and voice and to leave the painful memories in the past where she had tried so hard, for so long to leave them.

As she calmed down, Trace's strength backed off and his touch became gentle where it had been iron. He stroked her back softly and pushed her hair back from her face and gently tugged on it. His touch was cathartic, with his warm voice in her ear like a melody in the background, and she let herself almost drown in the sound as it drew her further and further from the mental and emotional anguish that had overwhelmed her earlier.

Physically she was exhausted by the thoughts and feelings that had come pounding back. Finally, she fell into the sweet oblivion of sleep there in his arms, safe from the terrors that threatened to crush her.

What Trace had just seen scared him. This beautiful, strong and resilient young woman that had withstood everything from the rigors of the trail to having to kill someone, had shattered right here in his arms tonight. He didn't know what she had started to read in the diary, but he had an idea that it involved the night that she had been attacked by the mob.

Mose had intimated that she had never dealt with it, but Trace had thought he was wrong, simply because she was so gracefully handling all of the stresses that she had been placed under. Feeling her come apart like this tonight made him understand that Mose had indeed been right. Frighteningly right. Someday she was going to have to figure out how to channel all of that terrible fear and pain. For right now, he was just grateful that they had made it through that in one piece at all. Jehoshaphat, she had been troubled!

He still held her to him, more gently than before, but firmly so that she'd know he was there protecting her even in her deepest sleep. He himself had shied away from dwelling on what had happened to her when she was attacked, and it had only touched him briefly and after the fact. The painful reality of it must have been horrific to still be affecting her this overwhelmingly this many months later.

He wondered again what kind of men could harm a beautiful, sweet young spirit like her. He had no idea how to even start to deal with something like this. He'd said that reading the journal had helped him understand her and it had. Now he just wished desperately that he could still interpret it so that he could understand this without having to put her through any more anguish over it.

As Trace held her to him so gently, he began to pray for guidance and strength. As hard as it was for him to deal with this, it must be nothing compared to her struggle. Hours later, when he finally felt like he could sleep, he was ultimately grateful that he couldn't read the journal anymore. It was enough to know that the memories could eat her alive without having to know all the horrible details of what that hellish night must have been like for her. All he truly needed to know was that she had been so deeply harmed by evil men and that she needed a greater power of good to shield her from it now.

Once again, as he finally drifted off to sleep, he wished desperately for the power that Josiah had blessed her with that day. That power could have brought her such needed comfort tonight.

Deep in the night he felt her begin to tremble again and her heart begin to race. Still somewhat asleep, he pulled her back into that tight embrace and began to talk to her. This time, she wasn't awake and he hoped that she didn't wake up. Being awake in this kind of fear would only make it seem all the more real and frightening.

He held her and stroked her, whispered gentle reassurances against her skin, and gratefully felt her relax back into him. He remembered that first nightmare that she'd had out on the trail. He wished he'd known then the kind of troubles that she'd been struggling with. He would have been able to help her better if he had.

Bringing her comfort was heaven. Holding her and touching her to dispel her fears was a mixed deal. Having her tight in his arms was wonderful, controlling himself was a bear. Even terrified, she was a very tempting entity. He pressed his lips to her brow and breathed in the sweet smell of her skin.

It was no wonder that he'd kissed her in his sleep that night. It was an almost overwhelming urge. Trying to think of anything other than how good she felt here in his arms, he wondered how he had ever been able to resist her these last months-and how he was going to be able to for the next couple of weeks until they had her safely back with her people.

The thought of leaving her behind to continue on to California was too hard to even begin to deal with tonight. He pulled her into his embrace even closer and pushed it completely out of his head for now. He couldn't bear to start heading there.

Giselle woke up in the darkness of the cave and wondered if it was morning yet. She couldn't see the pale crack in the ceiling, but her body felt like this night had lasted forever. She started to remember what had happened when she'd been reading to Trace the night before, and her mind shied away so hard that she felt herself wince. Even without reliving the memories, she knew that she'd pretty well come apart on Trace and had given him absolutely no explanation about why.

He still held her tightly against him. That strength and his willingness to be there for her even without understanding had been her salvation during those terrifying memories. How she wished that she had his strength all those months and months before. He had been an incredible comfort to her literally from the day that she'd met him. She rolled even tighter against him and sighed. Watching him drive away toward California was going to be the hardest thing she'd ever have to do.

Mentally shaking herself, she pushed the thought out of her head and literally chose not to think about that right now. Right now she needed to breathe in his security like life-giving air, and she didn't have the energy in her spirit to fight any other fights this morning. He was here beside her, sharing his ever steady, ever assuring stability with her, and for that she would be grateful all the days of her life.

This man had been a rock to lean on from that first night and had never let her falter even once. He wouldn't let her wobble here this morning either, and that knowledge brought her a sweet, healing peace that she let seep into her bones. She leaned her forehead against his chest, feeling almost overcome with gratitude. He had been her greatest gift ever, one that she would never forget.

Still mostly asleep, Trace felt her sigh against him. The tremulous fear was gone and the sound she had just made was a happy one, he was sure of it. He pulled her closer and ran a gentle hand down her back, unbelievably grateful that she was going to be okay. He should have known. She'd been so tough through this whole trip from the get-go. He thought back to all the things that she'd dealt with on this wagon trail and smiled sleepily. She was an incredible woman. It was no wonder that he'd fallen in love with her right from the start.

She stirred against him and looked up at him in the near dark of the cave and he saw her gentle smile. Leaning in, she kissed his chest and it made his heart trip for just a second. Her voice was tired, but peaceful when she whispered, "Thank you, Trace. Thank you for saving me again. I'm sorry that I got so upset last night. I didn't realize how Grandfather's journal would affect me. Please forgive me."

He pulled her head gently to him. "I'm sorry too, Elley. I would never have asked you to read it if I'd known. Please forgive me as well."

"Oh, Tracey. You have nothing to forgive." She shook her head. "You've been my best and dearest friend ever. No one has ever been as good to me as you. Thank you." She paused. "I feel like I owe you an explanation. But I don't think that I can really talk about things yet. Can I just tell you that the journal entry was about the night that the mob came and leave it at that?"

He wrapped both arms around her gently. "Of course, Elle. The last thing in the world that I want would be to make you upset. Please don't feel like you owe me an explanation. I absolutely understand. But can I tell you how proud I am of how strong you are? This whole trip you've amazed me. You are the strongest woman that I've ever known and I have a great respect for you."

Slowly, she let out a long sigh. "Thanks, Trace. That's the nicest thing I've ever been told, I think."

They lay there like that for a long time. Neither one of them wanted to move or speak for fear it would break the sweet spell that had been cast on the cave around them. As cold and treacherous as this last part of the trip would probably prove to be, this time together would be a treasured memory for both of them forever.

The crack in the ceiling did eventually lighten, but only slightly. Giselle got out of bed, started the fire, and peeked out of the blanket at the storm that had picked up again. It had been five days, and though the storm had calmed some in all that time, it had never cleared up even once. There was more than two feet of snow on the level. This morning the wind had strengthened and the snow that was piled up now blew sideways in a ground blizzard that left no visibility at all.

She could hardly see past the mouth of the cave in front of the stock and that white blur made her afraid. How were they ever going to get to the valley in all that? She turned and went back into the peace and security of the inner cave. She'd come back and milk and gather feed in a while. For now, she needed the warmth and shelter of the cave, even if it was just for her emotions.

Trace was up and dressed and starting to cook. She went and stood close to him. "That storm is raging again out there. Even the snow that has already fallen is back in the air."

He turned to her and hugged her to him. "It probably doesn't seem like it, but that will be a blessing. The wind will scour off the ridges and drift the snow into banks and it will actually make the trip out easier. We'll try to find a trail the wind has blown off and at nights we'll dig into the huge drifts and stay in a snow cave if we have to. The snow actually makes good insulation, believe it or not."

She gave him a squeeze. "I'm so glad that it's you that I'm stranded with, Trace. You're so smart about so many things. How did a doctor learn all this stuff about being a frontiersman?"

Laughing as he flipped the hot cakes, he admitted, "You should have seen me on my first trip across. We were blessed to be traveling with some old campaigners or we'd have never made it. The first time a party of Indians came into our camp, they were positively frightening. I would never have figured out how to handle them without watching those old mountain men. They were nothing like the tame natives that I grew up with in Georgia."

"How many times have you made this trip across?"

"This is the fourth time over, and obviously three trips back. Mose and I wanted to see some of the country and come to where slavery and the Blacks weren't such volatile issues and it's been good for both of us. I miss my parents a great deal, but the people out here are certainly more tolerant and less prone to prejudice."

As she set the table she mused, "Hopefully, the Mormons will find more peace out here as well. The hatred back in the States, and even in other countries, has been terrible. I never understand what makes people, that profess to be Christians, hate others because their belief in Christ differs. That seems so backwards to me."

"You're right, Giselle, but think back even to the people of the Bible. The devil has always used religion to promote hatred and persecution. Even some of the most devout persecuted the prophets thinking that they were heretics. Look at Paul. He was a great man, but at first he just didn't understand. He truly believed that the apostles were wicked."

She paused with a fork in her hand. "Thank goodness that he finally figured it out. Perhaps, in time, the people in our time will as well."

Trace shook his head. "I wouldn't count on things going without a bump even out here, Elley. Smooth sailing has never been the path of the believers and I honestly don't think that it ever will be. Lucifer has too much at stake to take his minions and back off. If what you believe truly did happen and Joseph did see the Father and the Son, then Satan has more of a vested interest in stopping this work than ever before. Even the Saints themselves will lose sight of the goal and persecute each other sometimes. That's the nature of man, I'm afraid."

"You're right. I already know that. The gospel is perfect, but we Saints certainly are imperfect mortals." She sighed. "Sometimes I dread the whole thought of being a second wife out here. Sometimes the Mormon women don't really like me. At least some of the ones whose husbands showed an interest in me."

Trace turned to stare at her. "What? What did you just say?"

She shook her head. "I was just agreeing with you about the Saints not always acting saintly to one another. As a whole, they are a great people, but there have been times that I haven't been treated all that Christlike right within the fold. The whole plural marriage concept has been particularly difficult. In the first place, it's an issue that is terribly hard to deal with. At least for me it has been.

"I hate the whole idea with a passion, even when I concede that God knows and understands what I don't. The actual implementation isn't very pretty. First wives don't tend to welcome younger, more uhm... What is the word? Let's just say women that haven't been so worn by time and hard work. There was a brother in Nauvoo that took a particular interest in me, and I believe that his wife hated me on sight. It was quite intimidating."

Trace narrowed his eyes questioningly as he looked at her. "Plural marriage? The Mormons really do practice polygamy? And you're all right with that?" He looked horrified.

Calmly Giselle continued to set the table. "Some of the Saints do engage in polygamy. I don't understand it, but I do know that the brethren believe it to be a divinely inspired concept. For me, I have finally had to simply concede that to me, it's abhorrent, but that God is all knowing, and that somehow I'm just missing the point with my small mortal mind. So no, in a way I am definitely not alright with it, but at some point I will have to come to grips with it, because marriage is a huge part of God's plan. There are far more women that have joined the Church than men."

She placed butter and preserves on the table and said tiredly, "Why do you think that I worry so much about getting so attached to you? I'm going to miss you miserably when you go. Besides that, I'm going to have to find a way to go from being with a man as attractive as you to facing marrying someone much less desirable. The idea is so repugnant that I already feel like a rebel whose soul is slated forever for fire and brimstone."

He was staring at her with his mouth open in shock, and neither one of them noticed that the hotcakes were smoking on the griddle. Finally, Giselle began to squirm under his stare. "While we're discussing the ugly truths of my religion, I should tell you that there's another concept that's even harder to understand for someone that believes that God is no respecter of persons." She looked down at her nervously clasped hands. "Blacks can't hold the priesthood either."

She struggled with her emotions for a few seconds and felt the tears escape from her eyes and trail down her cheek. "That's the hard one for me. I can't understand that for anything, but it's true. That one is far harder for me to deal with than plural marriage."

In the silence, they both noticed the smoking griddle at the same moment and Trace hurriedly scooped up the torched hot cakes, went to the curtained doorway, and threw them far out into the falling snow. He turned around and looked hard at Giselle as he went back to the fire. Shaking his head, he said, "Jehoshaphat! I'd heard that the Mormons practiced polygamy, but after meeting you and your grandparents, I never dreamed it was true! How in the world can you believe in your church when they do things like that?"

She looked at him steadily and finally said simply, "I believe that Joseph Smith truly did see the Father and the Son that day, Trace. I truly, honestly do."

He returned her straightforward look for several seconds before going back to making breakfast, and the silence stretched out between them for minutes. When he finally brought the plate to the table and sat across from her, they both bowed their heads without saying anything and Trace quietly asked a blessing on the food. For a little while, they both just ate, neither one of them voicing his or her own thoughts until at length Trace asked her, "Why do you believe that, Giselle? That he saw them?"

"Because when I first learned of the Church and its teachings, I had such a good feeling about it that I had to find out. I asked God if this really was His gospel and He told me yes."

Trace stopped chewing in the middle of his bite as he stared across the table at her. He watched her, almost studied her for a time again, and then shook his head. "Can't argue with that one, can you?"

They finished eating and cleaned it up together. Then she milked while he cut twigs for the stock to eat. They were both still quiet when they went back inside, and after a while, Trace lay back down and she sat in the rocker with her messy knitting in her lap. Her mind was far more occupied with her thoughts of him and what he was thinking about the Church, and sometimes she would go several minutes without a single stitch. Realizing it, she glanced down at the tangled lump in her lap and had to smile. She wasn't good at knitting and she wasn't fast either.

The look she had seen in Trace's eyes when he'd asked how she could believe in a church that practiced plural marriage was so depressing. She had so hoped that she and her grandparents had been good enough examples that someday he'd want to become a member, but after seeing his face, she didn't think that was even a remote possibility. He'd looked at her with a strong mixture of disbelief and disgust.

She could hardly blame him. She'd struggled with this idea from the very first time she'd ever heard it. Having more than one spouse seemed completely opposed to the way human nature felt about a spouse. At least it did to her. She couldn't imagine sharing a husband or being shared either.

And the Blacks holding the priesthood would be just as hard for Trace to cope with. She knew that without even asking. His friendship and respect for Mose had been unmistakable from the first night she'd met them. She thought about it for a few minutes and came back to the same place that she always did. God knew more than she did and she just had to have faith and try to be obedient even if she didn't understand. Looking over at Trace lying there asleep, she knew that marrying any other, whether she was the only wife or not, was going to be a problem for her for the rest of eternity.

She sighed and chastised herself. God was all powerful. She needed to trust in that to help her do what this life would ask of her. He wanted her to be happy. She truly believed that, so she just needed to be faithful and hold to the rod. In the meantime, they would need warm stockings, even if they weren't all that beautiful, and she set to knitting again with a purpose.

When Trace got up, he began to unload the things from the wagon, sort out what they would need to carry out and to pack the rest neatly into the back of the far cave. From time to time, he asked Giselle questions about what they would take, but other than that, their communication was rather limited. By the time that they went to bed that night, they were both tired and Giselle was more than a little discouraged. The idea of polygamy must really bother him.

CHAPTER 15

As Trace lay down beside her that night, he was bothered. It wasn't necessarily the idea of polygamy as much as the idea of Giselle being married to someone else at all that troubled him. He knew that she was worrying about them saying goodbye and how hard it would be, and she'd been diligent about not letting him get too friendly, but that didn't stop him from wishing that they weren't going to tell each other goodbye soon. He worried about telling her goodbye as well, but for him it made him want to cherish every second with her and hold her all the more. It was an emotion that definitely picked up steam when he was lying beside her.

It was Trace that woke up that night when he was kissing her neck in his sleep. He hadn't awakened her, but he wanted to and wanted her to kiss him back. He groaned and dragged himself out of the bed and stoked up the fire again. Then he sat in front of it, staring into the dancing red and orange flames.

For weeks now, he'd been toying with the idea of becoming a Mormon. Right up until this morning, everything that he'd learned had made sense and, it felt good in his heart, but the two ideas they'd talked about today had clobbered him. The polygamy possibly fit in a little if you considered Abraham and some of the prophets of old, but that racist stuff killed him.

Even in the Bible when it spoke of the Jews being the chosen people it had bothered him. The Father that he imagined wasn't racist. He knew in his heart that He wasn't, so how did all of this work? He picked up Giselle's Book of Mormon off the floor of the cave near their bed and turned it over and over in his hands.

She had said that it all came down to asking. At first that had seemed too simplistic, but on thinking about it, who could question God if you were sure of His answer? Not Giselle, and certainly not him. He put the book back down and went back to the fire to watch it dance and glow against the wood and embers. Giselle had been right again. He needed to ask.

He spent a quiet hour there in front of the flames, praying and thinking about the concepts that he had been learning over the last months from that beautiful girl sleeping there on the floor. She had been the best of Christian examples to him always, and so had her grandparents. They had a sweet spirit about them that had made them fairly glow. It was unmistakable and didn't leave much to doubt.

Thinking as he was, he was grateful to his parents, and even to Mose's real parents, for their guidance and teaching throughout his life about his Father in Heaven. It had been a foundation for his everyday living that had helped him avoid so many of the pitfalls in this life that many of the men around him had fallen into. On looking back, he could easily see how living an honorable, Godly life had made for a much happier existence for him than for some other men.

He stood up and yawned and stretched. He was tired enough that, hopefully, he could go back to bed and keep his mind off of Giselle. Especially if he continued to ponder about God. That should help him. He slid in next to her and kept his distance except for putting his foot gently against hers. Just that little bit of contact was all that he needed. He smiled into the dark, remembering that first night that she had brought her bedroll to his wagon. Looking back over the months, he was really, really glad that she had done that.

He'd planned to keep his distance, but by morning he had her wrapped in his arms again. She was turned into him and didn't seem to mind being cuddled against his chest, and he just held her against him as he mentally began to plan for this day. He could still hear the wind and knew that the storm hadn't broken yet, but they needed to be getting packed and ready to get out of here the second that it did. The snow was deep and it would be a treacherous and grueling trek, but staying here any longer than they had to was a recipe for disaster and they both knew it. The winter would only get more and more cold and deep.

With that thought in mind, he held her and watched her sleep for a few more minutes. Then he gave her the softest of kisses on the top of her head and slipped out of the blankets again.

After stoking the fire, he dressed warmly and went out to care for the stock. Then he stopped and cut a number of stout willow lengths to start fashioning snowshoes for the two of them. This was another of the things that he had learned from that first trail across with the seasoned woodsmen. Their tutelage had been indispensable any number of times over the last three years, and he would always be grateful to them.

When Giselle woke up, she looked across to see Trace busily working on something at Petja's table. She could see willow sticks and strips of leather or rawhide, and he worked at whatever it was with a determined focus. She lay there and watched him for a while, marveling at how lucky she had been in finding his train to come across with that July day months ago. He was definitely not your average male, and his character traits and knowledge had been gifts to her time after time on this journey.

She slipped silently out of the blankets and knelt to say her morning prayers, knowing that giving thanks for Trace would be a good part of her prayer. He had grown to be the most important part of her life. She stood up and took her clothes into the back cave to dress quickly, mentally going over what she needed to be doing today to get ready to leave as soon as the weather broke.

As Trace worked on his snowshoes, he heard a sound and looked over at the bed to see Giselle kneeling there in her white nightgown. She almost looked like an angel in spite of her dress, and he watched her for a moment in fascination. Even through months of the trail and sickness and hardship, she was still the most beautiful woman that he had ever seen, both inside and out, and she amazed him sometimes that she had been able to stay that way through it all. The hardships had made her even more beautiful to him in a way, because he knew of the substance and character strength that lay beneath the beautiful bone structure and figure. She stood up and he looked back to his snowshoes.

He knew this last leg of the journey was going to be the most trying of all, but still he wished that their time together wasn't almost gone. For about the ninetieth time, he wondered if there wasn't some way that they could stay together, but it always came down to the fact that he had committed to going all the way to California and was not a man that went back on his word. And she had given up everything in her whole life to make this journey to the Mormon Zion, and he wasn't a member of her church anyway. At least not yet. Maybe he could come back to her valley next spring and she would still be unmarried. The very thought of her married to someone else, especially as a second wife, made him feel as ornery as that darned rogue mule.

That day, Trace finished moving all but the last few things that they'd need out of the wagon and stored them inside the cave. They took the money out of the false bottom, packed it securely in a leather bag, and stuffed it down into a bag of dried beans for the trip. Then Trace began to painstakingly wall off the back section of the cave with the chunks of rock that lay nearby. He finished the snowshoes, made a rough cloak for her out of the elk hide that Many Feathers had given her, and then fashioned packs for the mules and both of them to use on the walk out. He made her some fur lined mittens and rough boots for both of them out of the bear hide. They weren't beautiful, but they would keep them from getting frozen feet at least.

Giselle finished the long awaited stockings, and they laughed together at how funny they looked before she packed them away and did a last washing of their clothes. She was going to have to leave most of her things here in the cave, and some little quirk of her personality demanded that she leave them all clean in case they didn't stay packed in the back cave as they hoped. The idea of someone getting into her under things was very troubling to her. She washed everything, then took her underclothes out and hung them from the hoops of the wagon cover so that she didn't have to face Trace weaving in and out of her undies hanging inside with their outerwear. He laughed at her again when he realized what she was doing out there. By that evening, they were dead tired, but ready to go except for the last few things that they'd need right up until the last minute.

Somehow, both of them knew that this would be their last night together there in the peace and warmth of the cave, and primitive as it was, it had been a happy home for them for these seven days. They'd been warm and snug and more together than they'd been the whole journey because of the days spent lounging and reading and talking. That night there was almost a feeling of melancholy as they banked the fire and blew out the candle. Even though they knew that they would be saying goodbye soon, both of them snuggled together tightly for this last precious time of just the two of them. They didn't talk much after they prayed together, just lay there together like spoons for a long time before finally dropping off to sleep.

The silence of the cave was almost eerie after the constant wind of the last week. The crack in the ceiling was a stark, bright line and they knew that the storm had finally blown itself out. With the clear skies, the temperature had plummeted and the cave was colder this morning than it had been since they'd been there. Trace lit their last fire and began milking the cow. Giselle went out to the wagon to gather up the last of her laundry that she'd left hanging there.

She climbed the wagon wheel and slung a leg over the wagon box and pushed through the flaps to come face to face with Many Feathers. He was standing there with one of her chemises in his hands and all thought of thanking him for his help in finding the caves disappeared in outrage at finding him there with her lingerie. She went to snatch the chemise out of his hands and he evaded her grab. It made her hopping mad in an instant. She tore into him and went off like a little, Dutch stick of dynamite.

She snatched at the chemise again, and this time, she caught it and began whacking him with it as she gave him a piece of her mind. How dare he be in here with her underwear! He didn't say anything, didn't even change his expression, and it made her madder than ever and she actually went to hit him with her hand. Still without any change in his expression, he caught her arm before she connected and just held it so that she couldn't hit him. She didn't think that she could get any madder, but having him control her ticked her off even further and she stomped her foot at him in fury.

In that moment, Trace stuck his head inside the wagon flaps and looked at the two of them, wondering what in the world was going on. Giselle started to tell him about this incredible travesty of having this savage rummaging through her undies, but Many Feathers turned to Trace, and still holding Giselle's arm so that she couldn't hit him, he quietly spoke to Trace. Then dropped her arm, and without changing his expression, hopped out of the back of the wagon. Without looking back at her, he strode to his horse, mounted, and kicked the horse into a trot, and rode off.

Giselle was completely nonplussed when Trace began to laugh. He laughed and leaned over and rested his hands on his knees and laughed all the harder. He looked up at Giselle and laughed again so hard that tears started up and he couldn't seem to help himself. He laughed like he'd never heard anything so funny in all his days. Now Giselle was even getting mad at him. What did he think was so amusing?

She put her hands on both hips and gave him the look and he went off busting up again. This time she stomped her foot at him and he laughed until he could hardly breathe. Then he turned and headed back into the cave, still laughing like he had heard the funniest thing in the world. Giselle couldn't help herself and had to smile at him as she gathered up her underpinnings. What had Many Feathers said to Trace to crack him up like that?

Back in the cave, she began to fold her laundry and asked, "What did he say?" At her question, Trace went off again; holding his sides like they hurt from the humor. Giselle came over to him and put her hands back on her hips. "Trace Grayson, what did he say to you?"

Struggling to control his laughter was still hopeless and it was several seconds before he could even breathe, let alone tell her. Finally, he wiped his eyes and pulled her to him in a hug and started, "He said..." He busted up yet again and she had to wait one more time until he could speak. "He said that he'd changed his mind and that I could have you!"

Trace tried to keep his composure but it was hopeless, and he finally leaned over with his hands on his knees again and laughed until he cried, and she finally laughed with him. "Aaah, you two were the funniest thing I've ever seen!" He turned aside and went back to making breakfast, but every few minutes he'd belt out laughing again and say, "I can have you." And then shake his head.

When they went to eat, he still couldn't even pray without busting up, and Giselle had to take over mid-prayer. When he finally got control of himself, he sighed and said, "It's a good thing you have that hot, little, Dutch temper! He'd have followed us right into the valley and stayed with you there, and I was starting to seriously consider selling you." He paused and then mused, "I wonder how many horses he'd have gotten up to if you hadn't gone off on him out there." She gave him another look and then he laughed yet again.

They finished breakfast, packed up their gear, said a prayer to ask for help on the trip, and as they went out the cave opening, he hugged her to him again and said, "Come, Giselle, my little, Dutch spitfire. We must take you home to Zion."

He shook his head again and laughed. "I can have you." Still chuckling, he took her mittened hand in his and then took the lead line to the stock in the other and they set out across the pristine, white snow.

Chapter 16

At first the snow was deep and the mules and cows struggled so much that Trace eventually let go of her hand so that she could stay clear away from their floundering. Soon, however, they reached a windblown area and Trace helped her onto the trustworthy mule's back and then climbed up behind her. The rogue mule held their bedding and camp gear and the chickens had been strapped to the milk cow. The calf struggled far more than the others because it was shorter, even though Trace had left it free of any pack to reserve its energy. Dog, who was light enough to stay on top of the snow, brought up the rear.

Looking back over their ragtag pack string, he laughed again, near her ear. "We're the strangest group I've ever seen, I'm afraid."

She leaned back into his arms. "Strange is fine, just as long as we're making progress."

He hugged her. "It's going to be a hard trip, Elle. We may have to either eat them or leave them all behind, but I promise you that at least you and I are going to make it safely to your valley."

She thought about that and said, "You know what, Trace, I absolutely believe you. I've never doubted that since the time that you told me we'd make it even if we had to walk. I should never have worried. I've always been safe and secure with you."

It was a hard day. From time to time, they had to walk across the snow on their snowshoes. Sometimes they rode, and for a long time, they even rode along in the little stream that flowed down the valley. It was free of snow and shallow, and except for when it got too brushy, it was the easiest route of all. They were still in a country of rolling sage-covered hills, but the valley they traveled was slowly getting higher-walled as they progressed.

By the time the sun began to sink in the west, they were all exhausted and when they finally stopped for the evening, the animals just stood with their heads hanging while they started a cook fire and dug a cave-like hole into a drift. At first Giselle was afraid that they'd freeze or that the snow would collapse on them, but Trace pulled her close and prayed with her and, when he went right to sleep, she was reassured and snuggled over and followed suit. In the morning when she woke up, snug and warm beside him, she was frankly pleasantly surprised.

The second day was harder. There were more places that they had to slog through the deep snow, and by that night, both humans and beasts were completely drained. They slept in another snow cave, and then the next morning, Trace stopped where the wind had blown some grass clear and let the stock graze for more than an hour. After another grueling day, they found a small cave near the creek bank and built a fire in the mouth and spread out their bedding inside.

It wasn't as warm as the snow caves, but still Giselle liked it better. The snow caves made her feel like she couldn't breathe for some reason. Giselle asked Trace that night if they were making the headway that he had wanted, and he hesitated before he answered, "Yes and no. I knew it would be hard, and we're going to have to give the stock more time to feed when we find it, but we're doing okay. I had hoped to be able to go faster, but we can only do our best. We're still going to be fine. We are."

As they hiked or rode along, she watched the skies, wondering when they'd get hit with another storm. They actually had clear skies for most of four days before the low, gray clouds blew in. The temperature wasn't so bitter cold, but the wind blowing the snow in their faces was miserable, and when they came upon a cut bank that backed up to the wind direction, Trace stopped for the night even though it was only mid-afternoon. He tied the stock near the stream where the feed was plentiful and set about building a lean-to up against the dirt bank.

Cooking dinner seemed to take forever in the swirling gusts, and they eventually just ate their biscuits and beans half cooked and crawled into bed. It was still cold, even close together, and they shivered the whole night through. It was still snowing when the sun came up and they probably would have just stayed put except that they were too cold. They got up, packed, and headed out. It was warmer on the mule's back where its body heat seeped up into them.

The canyon they were traveling through became narrower and deeper, and while it was more protection from the wind, the drifts were sometimes almost impassable. They dug into a snow bank that night and it was much warmer. They slept better and longer and were far more refreshed when they got back up, which was good because it was another blustery day. They traveled in the stream water again to avoid the snow drifts. It was longer because of the meandering, but it was still faster and easier than bucking the drifts. They could almost see the livestock losing weight and the mule they rode was definitely getting bonier.

On the sixth day, they made it out of the narrow canyon and had to cross a wide intersecting valley. They entered another canyon on the side. It wasn't as steep or narrow, but it must have been higher in elevation because the snow became markedly deeper.

Following the stream wasn't an option here, and they snow shoed with their packs while the mules and cows bucked through the drifts as well as they could beside them. It was a grueling go, and they had to stop often to let the stock rest and by late that afternoon they had only come a few miles for all their struggle. Trace found a hollow at the base of a huge old cedar tree, built a tent of sorts, and spread out their bedding inside. He tied the stock nearby and all four of them lay right down in the snow when they were unloaded.

During the night, the wind whipped the tarp that made up their tent, and the next morning they found their bedding covered in inches of snow. Although they'd stayed dry in their sleep, the bedding had become partially sodden, and as they traveled that day, it froze into solid wads. That night they were in a snow cave again, but with damp bedding they were so cold that even snuggled together they shivered the whole night through again. Mid morning of the next day, when he spotted a sizable cave, Trace stopped for the day and built a roaring fire to dry out their bedding. They let the stock eat in the creek bottom, and once their bedding was warmed through, they went right to bed in the middle of the afternoon to try to make up for their sleepless night the night before.

They slept right through, and in the deepest dark before dawn, Dog began to growl. At first, Giselle just thought that it was Many Feathers again, but then they heard coyotes and knew that they were after their snow-bound stock. Trace went out with the rifle and rescued the calf from them. The coyotes had been able to stay on top of the snow and to maneuver much more nimbly, and if it hadn't been for Dog, the calf would have been lost. As it was, she had to be patched up, and they wondered if she would make it this time through the last rigors of this trip.

That was the morning that they saw the first signs of travel over the road from the valley. Someone was ahead of them on the trail, and from time to time from high spots they could see either part of the trail or smoke coming from chimneys in the surrounding hills. Giselle was both thrilled and sad. These past days had pushed her beyond what she had thought she could handle and the thought of civilization at last was enough to make her think that she would live through this. Then she would remember that she had to tell him goodbye and she wished they were a thousand miles from the valley.

It was a good thing that there was light at the end of the tunnel because a storm hit that afternoon that was an arctic gale. Trace had seen it coming, but hadn't found anywhere that looked suitable to get the stock some shelter, and they kept on into the face of the driven snow for hours. When it was too dark to see, they gave up and burrowed into a snow cave and left the poor animals right out in it. Giselle felt terrible about it and prayed for them over and over when she stirred in the night. The next morning she wanted to be up and gone so that they could find a way to help the animals as soon as possible.

The storm still raged and all of them, man and beast alike, were covered with a layer of crusted snow over their hair and clothes within minutes. Visibility was next to nil and it was a stroke of luck that they found the opening to a mine in the canyon beside the trail. Trace herded the animals in and then brushed off Giselle's cloak and hair and went right back out into it to find firewood. He was gone so long, that she was starting to go look for him when he showed up with parts of two trees to burn. They started a fire near the mine opening, cooked a hot meal, and spread out their bed, unbelievably grateful to be in out of that blinding, wind-driven snow and ice.

As they went to lie down, Giselle asked, "How much further, Trace? Do you have any idea?"

He pulled her into his arms and thought about it and said, "I've only been to your valley one time. The other times we went a different route, but as far as I can remember, we should get there tomorrow or the next day. Unless the weather stays like this. If it does I think we should stay right here."

He met her eyes and she repeated, "Tomorrow or the next day." This was it then. They had almost made it, but that revelation broke her heart into pieces. She turned her back to him and snuggled close and tried not to let him know that she was crying. Tomorrow or the next day. It felt like the end of the world.

The wind died down in the middle of the night and it was so quiet that it woke both of them up. She knew he was awake, but she didn't say anything to him. She didn't have any idea what to say. Those months ago, his asking her to agree to marry him and then have it annulled had seemed like the perfect answer. Tonight it felt like the most cruel thing in the world.

193

She turned over and put her face against his chest. She should have been trying to talk him into staying married. Whether he was leaving or a member or not, she should have tried to make this wonderful friendship be strong enough to keep it a marriage, but now it was too late. She breathed against him and tried to memorize that smell. She wanted to be able to remember it for all the rest of her life.

Her mind kept repeating the phrase Good Bye over and over and it felt like a nightmare, but she knew that she was wide awake. Thinking that he had gone back to sleep, she pressed a tender kiss to his chest and got up out of the bed and stoked the fire. She went to look out of the front of the mine opening at the beautiful, still, cold night. It was too painful to stay there in bed beside him.

Knowing that her thoughts were going to make her an emotional wreck, she tried to organize a plan in her head for her life, both in the next few days and long term. She was basically alone in the world now, or would be when Trace headed out, and she needed to know what she was going to do with herself. She had some money of her own, so she should be able to support herself at least for a while.

Before, she had assumed that she would come to Zion and find a husband and settle down, but that wasn't an option anymore. At least not right off. Even if that's what the brethren recommended, there was no way that she could face something like that so soon after Trace. She was going to have to figure out how to get him out of her heart and head first. She'd have to find a house or have one built and eventually find a way to make a living until she could face marriage at some point.

She was standing there trying to figure out how to pick up the pieces when Trace came up to stand behind her quietly. He wrapped his arms around her shoulders and leaned his chin on her head and looked out at the snowy canyon with her. Neither one of them said anything. What could you say at a time like this?

They stood there until they were both shivering and then they turned and got back into bed, still without saying a word. Once there, Trace wrapped his arms around her like he never wanted to let go and she met him more than half way. It was like they had to fit the huge amount of emotion they were feeling into the short couple of hours before dawn.

Even staying in bed longer than usual didn't satisfy the emotional maw that they were in danger of falling into. She had never been so frustrated in her life when they strapped back on the snowshoes and started down the snowbound trail. The sun had come out in a glorious display of sparkling diamonds on the snow, and its blinding brightness felt like it was mocking them as they trekked along.

The visibility was boundless and they could see a person coming on the trail ahead of them for miles. It was a single person and a pair of pack mules, and it was like a clarion call that they were at the end of the trail.

They'd been watching the lone figure trudge along for hours, just like they were through the exhausting snow, when she heard Trace whisper, "Mose." He turned to Giselle. "That's Mose! I'd know that walk anywhere!" He put his fingers to his lips and let go a shrill whistle and within seconds the lone figure sent an answering whistle back. Dog took off bounding over the snow towards him and Trace turned and gave Giselle a huge, happy hug. "That's Mose!"

When they finally made it to him, watching this reunion brought tears to her eyes. These two were closer than brothers, and their happiness at seeing each other again was overwhelming. Giselle stood to the side for a second and then Mose turned to her and picked her up in another huge bear hug. "Miss Giselle. I had plumb forgotten just how beautiful you were. It's so good to see you made it!"

She laughed at him through her tears. "You never doubted that we'd make it, did you, Mose? You should know that Trace can do anything that he puts his mind to."

"That I do, Miss Giselle. That I do. I never doubted for a minute, I just wondered if you needed a little help is all. The weather turned off and I thought I'd come and bring you all some warm clothes and gear."

Trace slapped him on the back. "You old codger! We came through fine. Giselle is so tough that a little nasty weather is nothing. She just puts her face into the wind and heads out."

They talked and joked for a few more minutes and then turned and headed back the way that Mose had come. They got quieter as they got winded from the drifts in the trail; and by dark they were still a mile or more up the canyon, but decided to keep on walking and make it into town even if they got there in the middle of the night. The moon on the snow made seeing the trail reasonable, and even though she was dead tired, Giselle continued to place one foot in front of the other. When she started to drag, Trace came up to her and put an arm over her shoulder and said, "Just think, Giselle. A real bed, just a couple more hours away."

She looked up at him and into his eyes. With a smile that wasn't very convincing, she said, "That will be wonderful, won't it, Trace?"

He squeezed her shoulder. "Come on, Elle. You've wanted this for a long, long time. You're finally almost to Zion!"

She put a mitton up to pat his. "I know, Trace. And I am glad. I'm just tired." They'd made it to where the trail was somewhat packed down and Trace reached over and set her up on the mule again.

"You ride for a while then. We're almost there."

What time it was was anyone's guess when Mose led them to the boardinghouse rooms that he had arranged for on the eastern edge of the town. She was glad that she was too tired to dwell on how much her heart hurt when Trace walked her to the door of her room, told her goodnight and went back out to see to the stock before coming up to the room he would be sharing with Mose. It was the first time in more than four months that she hadn't had him beside her at night. Even tired as she was, it was awful to go to bed alone.

She slipped out of her clothing and between the warm sheets and tried to bask in the feel of real walls, floor, and furniture. It really was nice. So then why did she keep having to wipe at her eyes? And why was her pillow so damp all of a sudden?

Trace was up early in spite of being tired. For some reason he was having a hard time sleeping. He thought the reason had something to do with the look in Giselle's eyes as he'd said goodnight at her door last night. She'd looked more sad than tired, even after finally reaching her Zion.

He knew she had to meet with their prophet today, and it had been a pretty rough trip. Maybe nice clothes and a bath would help. He arranged for her to have bath water in an hour or two and he went out to find the general store. When he'd bought her new clothing, he stopped and checked on her stock and paid a boy to milk her cow and went back. He wasn't sure whether she'd be awake, but he knocked on her door anyway and was glad when she opened it right up.

She smiled a greeting, but her eyes were still sad. He walked in, laid the new clothes on the bed, and turned to take her into a hug. "Aren't you happy to finally make it to your Zion at all?"

She pulled back and went to look at the dress and other things he'd bought. "I'm happy. Just tired. How did you know what size to buy?"

He laughed. "I didn't. I just tried to describe you to the woman at the mercantile. I have no idea if they'll fit, but I knew that you hadn't brought much with us from the cave and that you have to meet with Brigham Young this morning. If these won't work, I'll hurry and exchange them for you."

Still looking at them, she said, "I think they'll fit. Will you come with me to meet with Brother Brigham, or are you in too much of a hurry to leave?"

"I'll go with you. When do you want to leave?" He pulled her toweling off of her head and began to play with her wet hair. "How long will it take you to tame this?"

She smiled up at him in the mirror of the dresser. "It might take a while. Give me forty-five minutes. It's a wreck. Have you already eaten?"

"No, but I'm starving. Hurry and we'll eat together." He left her there and went back out to find out where Mose had gone. He'd been asleep when he left, but now he was gone. He never did find him and, in fact, didn't see him until he and Giselle were having breakfast in the little dining room.

Mose walked up to their table with his big, white grin. "Well, well. You two don't even look like the same two snow monsters that I found yesterday out on that trail."

"Yes, well, a bath and shave and clean clothes will do wonders." Trace remarked placidly. "Where have you been? Have you eaten?"

"I've eaten and have already been about the town working on professional neighborly relations with the folks hereabout."

Trace smiled and asked, "What exactly does that mean, Mose? And what's with this mysterious smile you're wearing? You're looking very pleased with yourself this morning."

Mose glanced at Giselle quietly eating her breakfast and asked, "Do you remember that day last July when I told you that you looked goofy?" Trace grinned and nodded. "Well, this morning that's exactly how I feel."

"Oh really?"

Mose chuckled. "Actually, I've been this way for three days now. This goofy smile is positively stuck. I feel ridiculous." Giselle looked from one of them to the other, wondering what was going on.

Trace slapped Mose on the brawny shoulder. "Well, good for ya'all! Sit down and eat again and we'll go out and see what you've found."

Giselle took another bite and asked daintily, "I am confused. You found something that makes you feel ridiculous, Mose? What does this mean?"

Shaking his head and laughing, Mose said, "Oh, it's nothing, Miss Giselle. I just really like your Great Salt Lake town is all."

"Don't you believe him, Elle." Trace smiled at her. "From that look on his face, I'd say he's either robbed the Mormon bank or met a pretty girl."

She perked right up. "You met a girl, Mose? Here in Zion? What is she like?"

His grin split from ear to ear. "I met a girl and she is prettier than a new red wagon. You'll have to come and meet her."

Trace chuckled. "You're right. You're disgusting."

Giselle shook her head. "I don't think you're disgusting, Mose. I think you're *engelachtig* when you're in love. But what is this goofy? What does it mean?" They tried to explain it to her and she looked thoughtfully at Mose for a second and then said, "Yes, I think you are right. You look this goofy." They all laughed as Trace and Giselle finished their breakfast.

Mose went off again somewhere while Trace took Giselle and her package of money to Brigham Young. They found him in an office in the heart of the thriving community and his face lit up when he saw Giselle. Trace thought that he'd never met anyone so dynamic when he shook his hand heartily as she introduced him. He turned back to her. "Where are Josiah and Petja, Sister VanKomen?"

Her face fell as she had to tell him what had happened and he was genuinely saddened by her tale. He placed a huge and calloused hand on her shoulder. "I'm so sorry to hear about your grandparents, sister. They were most wonderful people.

I'm sorry that you've lost them. Where are you staying then if they are gone, now that you're in town?"

She made a dainty grimace. "I don't know for sure. We just got in late last night and I haven't gotten that far. I wanted to bring the money to you before we did anything else. Here it is and here is the list of what money is for what property. Most of it belonged to the Church itself."

"Yes, thank you for a job well done. Go to Bishop Syndergaard. He was your bishop back in the States, wasn't he?" She nodded. "Go to him and he will find you a place." He turned to Trace. "Now am I to understand that you are part of the teamster train that came in a week or two ago? Are you the man they were waiting for?"

"Yes, I believe that I am. Why?"

Brigham pulled out a pocket watch and glanced at it. "I regret that I have a meeting right now that I'm already late for. Is there any way that I could trouble you for some time to discuss a few things later this afternoon? Say two o'clock, maybe?"

"Certainly." Trace nodded. "Back here again?"

"Thank you, young man. Now if you will excuse me." He patted Giselle on the shoulder as he went out. "Once again, thank you, sister, for all that you've done, and I'm sorry for your loss." He bustled out and Trace felt like the air was sucked right out of the room when he went. What a powerful personality this man had.

They went out into the hall and looked at each other and Trace asked, "Where to now, sister?"

She smiled at him a little sadly. "To Bishop Syndergaard's, I guess." She looked down. "And we need to find out how to go about having our marriage annulled." She looked up at him. "When are you leaving? Do you know yet?"

He shook his head as he watched her eyes. "I haven't even talked to Mose or John about it. As soon as possible, I suppose. Where is this bishop's place?"

"Oh, I don't know. I forgot to ask. Someone will know, I'm sure."

They asked some people in the outer office and then Trace took her to a home near the general store and they did, indeed, find the man she was seeking. He welcomed her right in with a smile that nearly consumed his face and a veritable bear hug. He shook Trace's hand with vigor and slapped him on the back as he turned to go after promising that he'd bring the rest of Giselle's things by later when he knew what they had to do about their marriage. The look that passed between them felt like it cut Trace's heart right out, but he didn't know what else to do other than just turn and walk away. This had been the plan for over four months and he was already committed to leaving, but it was killing him. And from the looks of Giselle, she wasn't any happier about it than he was.

When Bishop Syndergaard's door shut firmly behind Trace, Giselle couldn't help the tears that began to slide down her cheeks. Embarrassed, she wiped at them stubbornly, but she couldn't stop them no matter how hard she tried. The kindly, old bishop led her through into the parlor and seated her on the sofa and asked gently, "Who was that young man, Sister VanKomen?"

Haltingly, she told him the whole story, from that first night with Filson down to telling Trace good bye just now. Hesitantly, she finished, "I'll be fine, Bishop. It's just going to take some time to get my heart over him is all. I'm sorry for being so emotional. I must be tired."

Gently, the bishop asked her, "If you love each other, why do you need to get over him?"

"Oh, Bishop. It's not all that simple. Annulling this marriage was the plan all along. And he has to leave and he's not a member and... And... And I don't even know what."

"Sister VanKomen. Or actually Sister Grayson, do you not understand that true and honest love like you two have is rare and sweet and precious? Our Father in Heaven wants you to be happy. If this man isn't a member yet, that doesn't mean that you have to get away from him. He's a good man. That's very apparent.

"Your Father in Heaven would much rather that you stay married to the good man that you are in love with than that you leave him to marry another that you feel nothing for. That's a recipe for disaster. For everyone that's involved. And trust me; this plural marriage business is hard enough without trying to go into it without love." He paused and continued. "Do you think that your husband will someday join the Church?"

She shook her head and the tears welled again. "He believes. At least I think that he does. But he can't abide that the Blacks can't be given the priesthood. And the plural marriage stuff is very troubling to him as well. I think if he was going to join, he would have already asked."

Bishop Syndergaard turned and walked to the window and back and then said, "Sister Grayson. You must make your own decisions, based on your own good judgment and prayer, but as your bishop, I think for you to walk away from this young man would be a mistake. You both obviously love each other. Is there any way that you can try to work things out?"

Hope flitted across her face. "I don't know. I assumed that you would want me to get away from him because he isn't a member. We haven't even talked about it."

"Well, my dear, marriage is vitally important to our Heavenly Father's plan, and strong ones are few and far between. When you are so in love with the husband you have, see what can be done to keep him, don't you think? Just don't give up hope that someday he'll want to be baptized. He seemed like a good man that would want to embrace truth."

Giselle stood up and hugged him. "Oh, thank you, Bishop! I don't know if it will work, but I'd love to be able to be with him!"

After dropping Giselle at her bishop's, on the way back to the boardinghouse, Trace tried to lighten up his attitude, but this all felt completely wrong. He shouldn't be planning to walk away from this girl. Somehow they could work out the kinks and find a way to stay together, couldn't they?

On the boardwalk ahead of him he saw some of the other teamsters that had been on the trip with them. They stopped him and asked how soon they were going to get away, and he assured them that John Sykes probably had a plan-talk to him. Trace knew he should find him as well, even though his heart wasn't in it. They might as well get going. The weather wasn't going to be getting any nicer if they waited. Finally reaching the boardinghouse, he turned in the door and went up the stairs to their rooms with a heavy heart.

Mose found him there an hour later, stretched out on the bed with a scowl. "So this is where you got to. I've been looking for you forever." He sat in the chair next to the window and quietly asked, "You're not really planning to go on to California and leave her are you?"

Trace made a disgusted sound. "Do I have any other options, Mose? This was the plan all along. I've committed to going and she's been trying to get here for almost two years. I'm not even a member of her church. I'm sure all those nice, old men that have welcomed her would be thrilled about that."

Mose went to tip back in the chair and Trace groused, "You're gonna break the chair, you big lout. Did you see your girl?"

Mose chuckled. "My, but aren't we a touch irritable this morning? I have a couple of pieces of information that you might be interested in. One is that Brigham Young approached John and asked him to sell the goods right here in Salt Lake City instead of moving on to California. He actually offered better prices than if we kept going."

Trace sat up on the bed and asked, "What did John tell him?"

"That he had to talk it over with you first. Apparently Brigham Young was waiting for some money to be brought in from the States, and it finally arrived today. Know anything about that?"

"Yeah. Josiah was bringing it. I didn't know anything about it until Giselle almost died. One day when she was so weak she asked me, if no one else made it, if I'd bring it to him."

"Well, it sounds like you brought the money to buy your own goods then. That is, unless you can't stand the thought of staying here with Giselle, and insist on leaving to travel over more snowy mountains."

"Oh, knock it off. It's bad enough without you hassling me. What else do you have to tell me?"

"Lucretia Tapp is in town. She came in on the stage, but her father sent a teamster train out here to sell as well. They actually planned to sell it here, but they didn't know about the Mormon health code. They brought wagon loads of tobacco and coffee and alcohol. No one's buying and she's not very happy about that."

"Have you talked to her?"

"She did actually speak to me. Just enough to ask where you were. It seems that you're the real reason for her being here."

"Oh, that's just great! Have you got any more such wonderful little tidbits of news? Or is that the last of it?"

Mose hesitated. "Well... just a little more. I'm joining their church."

Trace got up to pace the floor and said, "No, Mose. There are some things about their church that you don't understand. I seriously considered joining as well until Giselle told me a couple of things about it that are awful. They are racist. Blacks can't hold their priesthood. And not only that, but they really are involved in polygamy." He turned to look Mose in the eye. "I'm sorry to be the one to tell you. It looked good. It really did. It felt good and right until those."

Mose met his gaze. "I already knew about those things, Trace. And I don't understand them, but that doesn't change the fact that this is Christ's Church, headed by Him. They sound awful, I'll admit, but I asked if it was right." He paused. "I'm joining, Trace. I don't understand it all, but I'm going to trust God to take care of the things that don't seem right. I have to go with my gut here."

Trace just looked at him, questioning, and then sighed. "You're right, and I know it. I just hate the whole idea that the color of someone's skin would matter to God. I can't believe that. The God that I pray to is fair and honest. And the plural wives thing makes me sick."

Gently Mose replied, "Abraham did it. And a bunch of the others of the Bible. It's weird, but not unheard of. And remember there were times that only the tribe of Levi got the priesthood. For me, it just has to come down to faith. Once I knew that I was being told yes, I've just had to trust."

Trace went to the wash basin and splashed water on his face. "You stay here and trust. I have to go find out how to have a marriage annulled in this town." He sounded totally bitter and he didn't even care.

Mose caught his arm at the door. "What are you doing, man? I just told you that we can sell and stay here. You love that girl. Don't leave her!"

He shrugged out of Mose's grip. "I don't want to leave her, Mose. But that's been the plan. And we don't even know if we are staying for sure. She already has plans to move on with her life here. Some old idiot geezer wants her for his second wife."

"If he wants Giselle, he doesn't sound like an idiot to me. She's a grand girl. That's why you're going to stay married to her and live happily ever after."

Trace looked up at his friend. "You make it all sound doable, Mose, but I'm not sure that it really is."

Mose put a big finger into Trace's chest. "One thing's for sure, Trace. She's worth fighting for with everything you've got. Don't you give up on that girl. If you left here, you'd smash her heart into tiny pieces. And that girl's got a lot of heart. A whole lot of heart."

Trace just looked up at him until Mose nodded at the bed. "Get your boots on. Let's go talk to John. What, do I have to hold your hand through this? I have another hand that I want to hold now, you know. I don't want any part of California right now and neither do you."

They talked to John who was all for selling to the Mormons and staying put for the winter, except that a couple of the wilder teamsters wanted nothing to do with those blankety blank Mormons. John and Trace and Mose decided that they'd sell here and let the others do as they pleased.

With that decided, Trace took Mose with him to meet back with Brigham Young. Somehow Brigham had found out that Trace was a skilled doctor, and he wanted to find out what it would take to talk him into staying there in the valley on a permanent basis. Trace explained that he still had another year in Pennsylvania to truly be where he wanted to be as far as education. President Young offered to help pay for that education, and had several other options to try to talk him into staying there and practicing. Trace didn't commit to anything, but he had a head full of ideas when he went in search of Giselle that afternoon.

Back at Bishop Syndergaard's, they told him that she had gone with his wife to the general store and Trace headed there next. She wasn't there and he asked the proprietor if he had seen a pretty, young Dutch woman named Giselle. There was an older couple there and the man turned to Trace with a scowl and asked, "Who would be asking about Sister Giselle?" His wife looked livid at the question and Trace had to wonder if this was one of the men that wanted Giselle for his second wife.

The very thought made him furious and he turned to the man and very pointedly said, "Her husband would be asking. Is there a problem?" The man's mouth fell open in shock and his wife looked pleased. Trace probably shouldn't have done that. There was still the possibility that they would end up annulling their marriage, but he hadn't been able to resist. The whole idea of this man with his Giselle!

Just then, she walked into the store with an older, matronly woman. When she saw Trace, she came up to him with serious, wide, blue eyes. She looked at him and paused before she asked, "What did you find out, Trace?"

He glanced around them at the store and then said, "Could we go somewhere and talk, Elle?"

Still watching him, she said, "Sure, Trace. Is something wrong?"

He nodded. Something was definitely wrong. The whole idea of leaving her was terribly wrong. He just hoped that he could convince her of that. He took her elbow and led her out of the store. As they left, the older gentleman that had braced Trace looked at her almost coldly, while the wife looked mean and smug. Once outside, Trace said dryly, "I'm assuming he's one of the men that wanted to marry you." She grimaced and nodded. "No wonder you weren't very excited about the idea."

She paused and then said, "The gospel is perfect, Trace. It's just the people that aren't."

Outside the store it was cold and he asked her, "Are you warm enough if we just walk or should we go back inside somewhere?"

Giselle laughed up at him. "I'm wearing your stockings that I knitted. They aren't pretty, but they're very toasty. I'm fine. Are you?" He laughed with her and thought to himself, I'm fine when I'm with you, Elle. Just up ahead, he realized that Lucretia Tapp was approaching them on the boardwalk. Trace had never been so glad to have Giselle with him in his life. As she approached them, at first her face lit up, but then when she realized that Trace was with Giselle, she took on a pouty lower lip.

Trace stopped beside her on the walk. "Miss Lucretia, what a surprise. May I introduce you to my wife, Giselle? Giselle, this is a neighbor from back home in Georgia, Lucretia Tapp." Giselle smiled sweetly and dropped the smallest of curtsies. Trace subtly tugged on her hand and they continued on up the walk, leaving Lucretia standing on the boards, gaping behind them.

After a few more minutes of walking, Giselle glanced up at him. "She didn't appear too happy about you having a wife."

"Nope. Just about as happy as your suitor there in the store. I, on the other hand, have never been more grateful to be able to introduce you that way. Lucretia hasn't been the most pleasant experience of my life. Her father was the one that nearly killed Mose when he was seven, and he was Mose's wife's master."

Giselle put a gentle hand on his arm. "I'm sorry that you had to see her then, Trace. Does Mose know she's here?"

He nodded. "Mose is great though. He's learned to deal with her kind better than I'll ever be able to." They reached a vacant lot and Trace pulled her to a stop beside him.

Giselle looked up at him with big eyes. "What did you find out? About the annulment?"

Trace put up a hand and rubbed the back of his neck, but before he could admit that he hadn't even checked, she interrupted, "Trace..." She hesitated when he looked at her, dropped her eyes, and started again. "Trace, is there any way that I can go on to California with you?"

He looked down at her, puzzled. "What about coming to Zion, Elle? You've worked to get here for years. You wanted it more than anything."

Nodding up at him, she admitted, "I know. I did want it more than anything. But now I don't want it as much as I want to be with you. Could I go with you?"

He looked at her steadily. "I'm not going through to California anymore. Brigham Young is buying all of our goods here. He's been trying to talk me into staying here and practicing medicine."

She didn't say anything, just looked at him quietly, and he continued, "Mose wants to stay as well. He's joining your church, even though he can't hold the priesthood."

He looked down and then back up and then admitted, "I've been thinking about joining too. I believe that Joseph Smith saw the Father and the Son. I'm just trying to figure out how to deal with a couple of other things." She still didn't say anything, and he said, "Say something, Elle. Why are you not saying anything?"

Quietly, she said, "I'm wondering what you are thinking about me."

He took both of her shoulders in his hands. "Giselle VanKomen Grayson, I'm thinking that I love you."

He let her go and turned aside. "I know that I don't deserve you, Elle. You're such a good person. And I'm sorry that I'm not completely sure about the Church yet, but I love you. I'm in love with you. And I don't want to have our marriage annulled."

He turned back to her. "I want to be married to you really, Giselle. Not just in name. We're happy together. We work well together. We could make a great life. I'll die without you, Giselle." He paused again and searched her eyes. "I love you, Elley. Can I stay here with you and we'll be married? Really married?"

She was looking up at him, studying him intently, her eyes shining. He pulled her close to him and urged her, "Please say yes, Elley. It will kill me if you don't."

She hugged him tightly and finally broke the silence and went off talking excitedly, just as fast as she could. He listened for a minute, pulled back, bent, and kissed her for a long moment and then laughed, "English, Elle, English. I'm sorry, sweetheart, but I don't understand Dutch."

The End

About The Author

Jaclyn M. Hawkes grew up in Utah with 6 sisters, 4 brothers, and a number of pets. It was never boring! She earned a bachelor's degree, had a career, and travelled extensively before settling down to her life's work of being a mother of 4 magnificent and sometimes challenging children. She loves shellfish, the outdoors, and children and their laughter. She and her fine husband, their family, and their sometimes very large pets, now live in a mountain valley in Northern Utah, where it smells like heaven and kids still move sprinkler pipe.

To learn more about Jaclyn visit: www.jaclynmhawkes.com

To find other great books like
this one go to:

www.granitebooks.com